Lewis Carroll
Alice's Adventures in Wonderland

NOTES

丸橋 良雄
伊藤 佳世子

EIKO-SHA

ISBN 978-4-87097-129-5

（無料）音声ダウンロード URL
http://www.eiko-sha.com/saisei.html

Published
by
EIKO-SHA
5–6–5 Honkomagome, Bunkyo-ku, Tokyo 113-0021
Saimei-bldg 1F

はしがき

　Lewis Carroll（ルイス・キャロル、1832-98）は イングランド北西部チェシャー州ダーズベリ出身の数学者、写真家、作家、詩人である。本名は Charles Lutwidge Dodgson(チャールズ・ラトウィッジ・ドッドソン)で、作家として活動する時にルイス・キャロルというペンネームを用いた。母校オックスフォード大学で数学の講師を務めていたときに書き下ろした物語が *Alice's Adventures in Wonderland*(『不思議の国のアリス』)の原型となる。複数の語からなる造語など様々な実験的手法で注目されており、数学者としては、チャールズ・ドッドソン名義で著作を出している。彼の言葉遊びやロジック、幻想文学に対する才能は作品の出版以来多数の読者を惹き付けてやまず、依然として人気を博し続けており、その影響は児童文学の域に止まらずジェームズ・ジョイスのような20世紀の作家にも及んでいる。

　この物語が生まれたいきさつについて少し言及しておこう。1862年7月4日のよく晴れた午後に、ドッドソンは友人のロビンソン・ダックワースとともにクライスト・チャーチ学寮の学寮長であるリドル博士の三人の幼い娘たちをボート遊びに連れだした。この作品の冒頭に掲げられた詩からその時の様子がうかがえる。三人の姉妹は船尾に座って舵なわを膝の上にしっかりととり、彼女たちと向かい合ってダックワース（"the Duck"という名前で作品の中で登場する）、その後ろでドッドソンがのんびりと櫂をこいでいる。夏の日差しは強く、眠たくなるような午後であった。三姉妹の次女であるアリスはだんだん飽きてきて、詩にあるように a story "*with plenty of nonsense in it*"をしてくれと言ってきかない。そこで、ドッドソンが話し出したのが世界中に有名になった"Alice was beginning to get very tired of sitting by her sister on the bank, and of having nothing to do"という冒頭の言葉である。この題材をもとに手書きの『地下の国のアリス』が最初に書かれ、その後いろいろと手を加えられた。

この作品では、白うさぎの縦穴を通り抜けて、人間の世界へ落ち込んだアリスという名前の少女の物語が語られる。ノンセンス文学の系譜に属し言葉遊びが充満したこの作品にはドッドソンと友人たちに関わる逸話や、イギリスの児童が暗記させられる授業を風刺した比喩も数多く含まれている。不思議の国の論理で展開される物語は、世界中の多くの子供は言うまでもなく大人の間でも親しまれ続けてきた。挿絵は有名な挿絵画家であるSir John Tenniel(サー・ジョン・テニエル、1820-1914)が引き受け、1865年に『不思議の国のアリス』の初版本が出版された。

このテキストの原本はOxford English Novels版によった。英光社社長の藤平英一氏には編集上大変お世話になった。注釈そのほかの点については至らぬ点が多々あると思うが、そのような点については大方のご教示をお願いしたい。

平成22年4月
桜吹雪の舞う洛西にて

注釈者

丸橋良雄　伊藤佳世子

CONTENTS

	Lewis Carroll's Dedication	v
I	Down the Rabbit-Hole	1
II	The Pool of Tears	10
III	A Caucus-Race and a Long Tale	20
IV	The Rabbit Sends in a Little Bill	29
V	Advice from a Caterpillar	41
VI	Pig and Pepper	53
VII	A Mad Tea-Party	66
VIII	The Queen's Croquet-Ground	77
IX	The Mock Turtle's Story	89
X	The Lobster Quadrille	100
XI	Who Stole the Tarts?	110
XII	Alice's Evidence	119
	NOTES	130

LEWIS CARROLL'S DEDICATION

All in the golden afternoon
   Full leisurely we glide;
For both our oars, with little skill,
   By little arms are plied,
While little hands make vain pretence
   Our wanderings to guide.

Ah, cruel Three! In such an hour,
   Beneath such dreamy weather,
To beg a tale of breath too weak
   To stir the tiniest feather!
Yet what can one poor voice avail
   Against three tongues together?

Imperious Prima flashes forth
   Her edict 'to begin it'—
In gentler tone Secunda hopes
   'There will be nonsense in it!'—
While Tertia interrupts the tale
   Not *more* than once a minute.

Anon, to sudden silence won,
   In fancy they pursue
The dream-child moving through a land
   Of wonders wild and new,
In friendly chat with bird or beast—
   And half believe it true.

And ever, as the story drained
  The wells of fancy dry,
And faintly strove that weary one
  To put the subject by,
'The rest next time—' 'It *is* next time!'
  The happy voices cry.

Thus grew the tale of Wonderland:
  Thus slowly, one by one,
Its quaint events were hammered out—
  And now the tale is done,
And home we steer, a merry crew,
  Beneath the setting sun.

Alice! a childish story take,
  And with a gentle hand
Lay it where Childhood's dreams are twined
  In Memory's mystic band,
Like pilgrim's wither'd wreath of flowers
  Pluck'd in a far-off land.

CHAPTER I

Down the Rabbit-Hole

Alice was beginning to get very tired of sitting by her sister on the bank, and of having nothing to do: once or twice she had peeped into the book her sister was reading, but it had no pictures or conversations in it, 'and
5 what is the use of a book,' thought Alice, 'without pictures or conversation?'

So she was considering in her own mind (as well as she could, for the hot day made her feel very sleepy and stupid), whether the pleasure of making a daisy-chain
10 would be worth the trouble of getting up and picking the daisies, when suddenly a White Rabbit with pink eyes ran close by her.

There was nothing so *very* remarkable in that; nor did

Alice think it so *very* much out of the way to hear the
Rabbit say to itself, 'Oh dear! Oh dear! I shall be too
late!' (when she thought it over afterwards, it occurred
to her that she ought to have wondered at this, but at the
time it all seemed quite natural); but when the Rabbit
actually *took a watch out of its waistcoat-pocket,* and looked
at it, and then hurried on, Alice started to her feet,
for it flashed across her mind that she had never before
seen a rabbit with either a waistcoat-pocket, or a watch
to take out of it, and burning with curiosity, she ran across
the field after it, and fortunately was just in time to see
it pop down a large rabbit-hole under the hedge.

In another moment down went Alice after it, never
once considering how in the world she was to get out
again.

The rabbit-hole went straight on like a tunnel for some
way, and then dipped suddenly down, so suddenly that
Alice had not a moment to think about stopping herself
before she found herself falling down a very deep well.

Either the well was very deep, or she fell very slowly,
for she had plenty of time as she went down to look
about her, and to wonder what was going to happen next.
First, she tried to look down and make out what she was
coming to, but it was too dark to see anything; then
she looked at the sides of the well, and noticed that they
were filled with cupboards and book-shelves: here and
there she saw maps and pictures hung upon pegs. She
took down a jar from one of the shelves as she passed;

it was labelled 'ORANGE MARMALADE', but to her great disappointment it was empty: she did not like to drop the jar for fear of killing somebody underneath, so managed to put it into one of the cupboards as she fell past it.

5 'Well!' thought Alice to herself, 'after such a fall as this, I shall think nothing of tumbling down stairs! How brave they'll all think me at home! Why, I wouldn't say anything about it, even if I fell off the top of the house!' (Which was very likely true.)

10 Down, down, down. Would the fall *never* come to an end? 'I wonder how many miles I've fallen by this time?' she said aloud. 'I must be getting somewhere near the centre of the earth. Let me see: that would be four thousand miles down, I think—' (for, you see, Alice had 15 learnt several things of this sort in her lessons in the schoolroom, and though this was not a *very* good opportunity for showing off her knowledge, as there was no one to listen to her, still it was good practice to say it over) ' —yes, that's about the right distance—but then 20 I wonder what Latitude or Longitude I've got to?' (Alice had no idea what Latitude was, or Longitude either, but thought they were nice grand words to say.)

Presently she began again. 'I wonder if I shall fall right *through* the earth! How funny it'll seem to come 25 out among the people that walk with their heads downwards! The Antipathies, I think—' (she was rather glad there *was* no one listening, this time, as it didn't sound at all the right word) ' —but I shall have to ask them what the name of the country is, you know. Please, Ma'am, is this New Zealand or Australia?' (and she tried to curtsey as she spoke—fancy *curtseying* as you're falling through the air! Do you think you could manage it?) 'And what an ignorant little girl she'll think me for asking! No, it'll never do to ask: perhaps I shall see it written up somewhere.'

Down, down, down. There was nothing else to do, so Alice soon began talking again. 'Dinah'll miss me very much to-night, I should think!' (Dinah was the cat.) 'I hope they'll remember her saucer of milk at tea-time. Dinah, my dear! I wish you were down here with me! There are no mice in the air, I'm afraid, but you might catch a bat, and that's very like a mouse, you know. But do cats eat bats, I wonder?' And here Alice began to get rather sleepy, and went on saying to herself, in a dreamy sort of way, 'Do cats eat bats? Do cats eat bats?' and sometimes, 'Do bats eat cats?' for, you see, as she couldn't answer either question, it didn't much matter which way she put it. She felt that she was dozing off, and had just begun to dream that she was walking hand in hand with Dinah, and saying to her very earnestly, 'Now, Dinah, tell me the truth: did you ever eat a bat?' when suddenly, thump! thump! down she came upon a heap of sticks and dry leaves, and the fall was over.

Alice was not a bit hurt, and she jumped up on to her feet in a moment: she looked up, but it was all dark

overhead; before her was another long passage, and the White Rabbit was still in sight, hurrying down it. There was not a moment to be lost: away went Alice like the wind, and was just in time to hear it say, as it turned a
5 corner, 'Oh my ears and whiskers, how late it's getting!' She was close behind it when she turned the corner, but the Rabbit was no longer to be seen: she found herself in a long, low hall, which was lit up by a row of lamps hanging from the roof.

10 There were doors all round the hall, but they were all locked; and when Alice had been all the way down one side and up the other, trying every door, she walked sadly down the middle, wondering how she was ever to get out again.

15 Suddenly she came upon a little three-legged table, all made of solid glass; there was nothing on it except a tiny golden key, and Alice's first thought was that it might belong to one of the doors of the hall; but, alas! either the locks were too large,
20 or the key was too small, but at any rate it would not open any of them. However, on the second time round, she came upon
25 a low curtain she had not noticed before, and behind it was a little door about fifteen inches high: she

tried the little golden key in the lock, and to her great delight it fitted!

Alice opened the door and found that it led into a small passage, not much larger than a rat-hole: she knelt down and looked along the passage into the loveliest garden you ever saw. How she longed to get out of that dark hall, and wander about among those beds of bright flowers and those cool fountains, but she could not even get her head through the door-way; 'and even if my head *would* go through,' thought poor Alice, 'it would be of very little use without my shoulders. Oh, how I wish I could shut up like a telescope! I think I could, if I only knew how to begin.' For, you see, so many out-of-the-way things had happened lately, that Alice had begun to think that very few things indeed were really impossible.

There seemed to be no use in waiting by the little door, so she went back to the table, half hoping she might find another key on it, or at any rate a book of rules for shutting people up like telescopes: this time she found a little bottle on it, ('which certainly was not here before,' said Alice,) and round the neck of the bottle was a paper label, with the words 'DRINK ME' beautifully printed on it in large letters.

It was all very well to say 'Drink me,' but the wise little Alice was not going to do *that* in a hurry. 'No, I'll look first,' she said, 'and see whether it's marked "*poison*" or not'; for she had read several nice little

histories about children who
had got burnt, and eaten up
by wild beasts and other unpleasant things, all because
5 they *would* not remember
the simple rules their friends
had taught them: such as,
that a red-hot poker will
burn you if you hold it too
10 long; and that if you cut
your finger *very* deeply with
a knife, it usually bleeds; and she had never forgotten
that, if you drink much from a bottle marked 'poison,'
it is almost certain to disagree with you, sooner or later.

15 However, this bottle was *not* marked 'poison,' so Alice
ventured to taste it, and finding it very nice, (it had, in
fact, a sort of mixed flavour of cherry-tart, custard, pine-
apple, roast turkey, toffee, and hot buttered toast,) she
very soon finished it off.

* * * * *

20 'What a curious feeling!' said Alice; 'I must be shutting up like a telescope.'

And so it was indeed: she was now only ten inches
high, and her face brightened up at the thought that she
was now the right size for going through the little door
25 into that lovely garden. First, however, she waited for
a few minutes to see if she was going to shrink any

further: she felt a little nervous about this; 'for it might end, you know,' said Alice to herself, 'in my going out altogether, like a candle. I wonder what I should be like then?' And she tried to fancy what the flame of a candle is like after the candle is blown out, for she could not remember ever having seen such a thing.

After a while, finding that nothing more happened, she decided on going into the garden at once; but, alas for poor Alice! when she got to the door, she found she had forgotten the little golden key, and when she went back to the table for it, she found she could not possibly reach it: she could see it quite plainly through the glass, and she tried her best to climb up one of the legs of the table, but it was too slippery; and when she had tired herself out with trying, the poor little thing sat down and cried.

'Come, there's no use in crying like that!' said Alice to herself, rather sharply; 'I advise you to leave off this minute!' She generally gave herself very good advice, (though she very seldom followed it), and sometimes she scolded herself so severely as to bring tears into her eyes; and once she remembered trying to box her own ears for having cheated herself in a game of croquet she was playing against herself, for this curious child was very fond of pretending to be two people. 'But it's no use now,' thought poor Alice, 'to pretend to be two people! Why, there's hardly enough of me left to make *one* respectable person!'

Soon her eye fell on a little glass box that was lying under the table: she opened it, and found in it a very small cake, on which the words 'EAT ME' were beautifully marked in currants. 'Well, I'll eat it,' said Alice, 'and
5 if it makes me grow larger, I can reach the key; and if it makes me grow smaller, I can creep under the door; so either way I'll get into the garden, and I don't care which happens!'

She ate a little bit, and said anxiously to herself,
10 'Which way? Which way?' holding her hand on the top of her head to feel which way it was growing, and she was quite surprised to find that she remained the same size: to be sure, this generally happens when one eats cake, but Alice had got so much into the way of expect-
15 ing nothing but out-of-the-way things to happen, that it seemed quite dull and stupid for life to go on in the common way.

So she set to work, and very soon finished off the cake.

*　　*　　*　　*　　*

CHAPTER II

The Pool of Tears

'Curiouser and curiouser!' cried Alice (she was so much surprised, that for the moment she quite forgot how to speak good English); 'now I'm opening out like the largest telescope that ever was! Good-bye, feet!' (for when she looked down at her feet, they seemed to be almost out of sight, they were getting so far off). 'Oh, my poor little feet, I wonder who will put on your shoes and stockings for you now, dears? I'm sure *I* shan't be able! I shall be a great deal too far off to trouble myself about you: you must manage the best way you can;—but I must be kind to them,' thought Alice, 'or perhaps they won't walk the way I want to go! Let me see: I'll give them a new pair of boots every Christmas.'

And she went on planning to herself how she would manage it. 'They must go by the carrier,' she thought; 'and how funny it'll seem, sending presents to one's own feet! And how odd the directions will look!

> *Alice's Right Foot, Esq.*
> *Hearthrug,*
> *near the Fender,*
> *(with Alice's love).*

Oh dear, what nonsense I'm talking!'

Just then her head struck against the roof of the hall: in fact she was now more than nine feet high, and she at once took up the little golden key and hurried off to the garden door.

Poor Alice! It was as much as she could do, lying down on one side, to look through into the garden with one eye; but to get through was more hopeless than ever: she sat down and began to cry again.

'You ought to be ashamed of yourself,' said Alice, 'a great girl like you,' (she might well say this), 'to go on crying in this way! Stop this moment, I tell you!' But she went on all the same, shedding gallons of tears, until there was a large pool all round her, about four inches deep and reaching half down the hall.

After a time she heard a little pattering of feet in the distance, and she hastily dried her eyes to see what was coming. It was the White Rabbit returning, splendidly dressed, with a pair of white kid gloves in one hand and a large fan in the other: he came trotting along in a great hurry, muttering to himself as he came, 'Oh! the Duchess, the Duchess! Oh! won't she be savage if I've

kept her waiting!' Alice felt so desperate that she was ready to ask help of any one; so, when the Rabbit came near her, she began, in a low, timid voice, 'If you please, sir—' The Rabbit started violently, dropped the white kid gloves and the fan, and scurried away into the darkness as hard as he could go.

Alice took up the fan and gloves, and, as the hall was very hot, she kept fanning herself all the time she went on talking: 'Dear, dear! How queer everything is to-day! And yesterday things went on just as usual. I wonder if I've been changed in the night? Let me think: was I the same when I got up this morning? I almost

THE POOL OF TEARS

think I can remember feeling a little different. But if I'm not the same, the next question is, Who in the world am I? Ah, *that's* the great puzzle!' And she began thinking over all the children she knew that were of the same age of herself, to see if she could have been changed for any of them.

'I'm sure I'm not Ada,' she said, 'for her hair goes in such long ringlets, and mine doesn't go in ringlets at all; and I'm sure I can't be Mabel, for I know all sorts of things, and she, oh! she knows such a very little! Besides, *she's* she, and *I'm* I, and—oh dear, how puzzling it all is! I'll try if I know all the things I used to know. Let me see: four times five is twelve, and four times six is thirteen, and four times seven is—oh dear! I shall never get to twenty at that rate! However, the Multiplication Table doesn't signify: let's try Geography. London is the capital of Paris, and Paris is the capital of Rome, and Rome—no, *that's* all wrong, I'm certain! I must have been changed for Mabel! I'll try and say " *How doth the little—*" and she crossed her hands on her lap as if she were saying lessons, and began to repeat it, but her voice sounded hoarse and strange, and the words did not come the same as they used to do:—

> '*How doth the little crocodile*
> *Improve his shining tail,*
> *And pour the waters of the Nile*
> *On every golden scale!*

> *'How cheerfully he seems to grin,*
> *How neatly spread his claws,*
> *And welcome little fishes in*
> *With gently smiling jaws!'*

'I'm sure those are not the right words,' said poor Alice, and her eyes filled with tears again as she went on, 'I must be Mabel after all, and I shall have to go and live in that poky little house, and have next to no toys to play with, and oh! ever so many lessons to learn! No, I've made up my mind about it; if I'm Mabel, I'll stay down here! It'll be no use their putting their heads down and saying "Come up again, dear!" I shall only look up and say "Who am I, then? Tell me that first, and then, if I like being that person, I'll come up: if not, I'll stay down here till I'm somebody else"—but, oh dear!' cried Alice, with a sudden burst of tears, 'I do wish they *would* put their heads down! I am so *very* tired of being all alone here!'

As she said this she looked down at her hands, and was surprised to see that she had put on one of the Rabbit's little white kid gloves while she was talking. 'How *can* I have done that?' she thought. 'I must be growing small again.' She got up and went to the table to measure herself by it, and found that, as nearly as she could guess, she was now about two feet high, and was going on shrinking rapidly: she soon found out that the cause of this was the fan she was holding, and she dropped it hastily, just in time to avoid shrinking away altogether.

'That *was* a narrow escape!' said Alice, a good deal frightened at the sudden change, but very glad to find herself still in existence; 'and now for the garden!' and she ran with all speed back to the little door: but, alas! the little door was shut again, and the little golden key was lying on the glass table as before, 'and things are worse than ever,' thought the poor child, 'for I never was so small as this before, never! And I declare it's too bad, that it is!'

As she said these words her foot slipped, and in another moment, splash! she was up to her chin in salt water. Her first idea was that she had somehow fallen into the sea, 'and in that case I can go back by railway,' she said to herself. (Alice had been to the seaside once in her life, and had come to the general conclusion that, wherever you go to on the English coast you find a number of bathing machines in the sea, some children digging in the

sand with wooden spades, then a row of lodging houses, and behind them a railway station.) However, she soon made out that she was in the pool of tears which she had wept when she was nine feet high.

'I wish I hadn't cried so much!' said Alice, as she swam about, trying to find her way out. 'I shall be punished for it now, I suppose, by being drowned in my own tears! That *will* be a queer thing, to be sure! However, everything is queer to-day.'

Just then she heard something splashing about in the pool a little way off, and she swam nearer to make out what it was: at first she thought it must be a walrus or hippopotamus, but then she remembered how small she was now, and she soon made out that it was only a mouse that had slipped in like herself.

'Would it be of any use, now,' thought Alice, 'to speak to this mouse? Everything is so out-of-the-way down here, that I should think very likely it can talk: at any rate, there's no harm in trying.' So she began: 'O Mouse, do you know the way out of this pool? I am very tired of swimming about here, O Mouse!' (Alice thought this must be the right way of speaking to a mouse: she had never done such a thing before, but she remembered having seen in her brother's Latin Grammar, 'A mouse—of a mouse—to a mouse—a mouse—O mouse!') The Mouse looked at her rather inquisitively, and seemed to her to wink with one of its little eyes, but it said nothing.

'Perhaps it doesn't understand English,' thought Alice;
'I daresay it's a French mouse, come over with William the Conqueror.' (For, with all her knowledge of history, Alice had no very clear notion how long ago anything had happened.) So she began again: 'Où est ma chatte?' which was the first sentence in her French lesson-book. The Mouse gave a sudden leap out of the water, and seemed to quiver all over with fright. 'Oh, I beg your pardon!' cried Alice hastily, afraid that she had hurt the poor animal's feelings. 'I quite forgot you didn't like cats.'

'Not like cats!' cried the Mouse, in a shrill, passionate voice. 'Would *you* like cats if you were me?'

'Well, perhaps not,' said Alice in a soothing tone: 'don't be angry about it. And yet I wish I could show you our cat Dinah: I think you'd take a fancy to cats if you could only see her. She is such a dear quiet thing,' Alice went on, half to herself, as she swam lazily about in the pool, 'and she sits purring so nicely by the fire, licking her paws and washing her face—and she is such a nice soft thing to nurse—and she's such a capital one for catching mice—oh, I beg your pardon!' cried Alice again, for this time the Mouse was bristling all over, and she felt certain it must be really offended. 'We won't talk about her any more if you'd rather not.'

'We, indeed!' cried the Mouse, who was trembling down to the end of his tail. 'As if *I* would talk on such a subject! Our family always *hated* cats: nasty, low, vulgar things! Don't let me hear the name again!'

'I won't indeed!' said Alice, in a great hurry to change the subject of conversation. 'Are you—are you fond—of —of dogs?' The Mouse did not answer, so Alice went

on eagerly: 'There is such a nice little dog near our house I should like to show you! A little bright-eyed terrier, you know, with oh, such long curly brown hair! And it'll fetch things when you throw them, and it'll sit up and beg for its dinner, and all sorts of things—I can't remember half of them—and it belongs to a farmer, you know, and he says it's so useful, it's worth a hundred pounds! He says it kills all the rats and—oh dear!' cried Alice in a sorrowful tone, 'I'm afraid I've offended it again!' For the Mouse was swimming away from her as hard as it could go, and making quite a commotion in the pool as it went.

So she called softly after it, 'Mouse dear! Do come

back again, and we won't talk about cats or dogs either, if you don't like them!' When the Mouse heard this, it turned round and swam slowly back to her: its face was quite pale (with passion, Alice thought), and it said in a
5 low trembling voice, 'Let us get to the shore, and then I'll tell you my history, and you'll understand why it is I hate cats and dogs.'

It was high time to go, for the pool was getting quite crowded with the birds and animals that had fallen into
10 it: there were a Duck and a Dodo, a Lory and an Eaglet, and several other curious creatures. Alice led the way, and the whole party swam to the shore.

CHAPTER III

A Caucus-Race and a Long Tale

They were indeed a queer-looking party that assembled on the bank—the birds with draggled feathers, the animals with their fur clinging close to them, and all dripping wet, cross, and uncomfortable.

The first question of course was, how to get dry again: they had a consultation about this, and after a few minutes it seemed quite natural to Alice to find herself talking familiarly with them, as if she had known them all her life. Indeed, she had quite a long argument with the Lory, who at last turned sulky, and would only say, 'I am older than you, and must know better'; and this Alice would not allow without knowing how old it was, and, as the Lory positively refused to tell its age, there was no more to be said.

At last the Mouse, who seemed to be a person of authority among them, called out, 'Sit down, all of you, and listen to me! *I'll* soon make you dry enough!' They all sat down at once, in a large ring, with the Mouse in the middle. Alice kept her eyes anxiously fixed on it, for she felt sure she would catch a bad cold if she did not get dry very soon.

'Ahem!' said the Mouse with an important air, 'are you all ready? This is the driest thing I know. Silence all round, if you please! " William the Conqueror, whose

cause was favoured by the pope, was soon submitted to by the English, who wanted leaders, and had been of late much accustomed to usurpation and conquest. Edwin and Morcar, the earls of Mercia and Northumbria—"'
'Ugh!' said the Lory, with a shiver.
'I beg your pardon!' said the Mouse, frowning but very politely: 'Did you speak?'
'Not I!' said the Lory hastily.
'I thought you did,' said the Mouse. '—I proceed. "Edwin and Morcar, the earls of Mercia and Northumbria, declared for him: and even Stigand, the patriotic archbishop of Canterbury, found it advisable—"'
'Found *what?*' said the Duck.
'Found *it*,' the Mouse replied rather crossly: 'of course you know what "it" means.'
'I know what "it" means well enough, when *I* find a thing,' said the Duck: 'it's generally a frog or a worm. The question is, what did the archbishop find?'
The Mouse did not notice this question, but hurriedly went on, '"—found it advisable to go with Edgar Atheling to meet William and offer him the crown. William's conduct at first was moderate. But the insolence of his Normans—" How are you getting on now, my dear?' it continued, turning to Alice as it spoke.
'As wet as ever,' said Alice in a melancholy tone: 'it doesn't seem to dry me at all.'
'In that case,' said the Dodo solemnly, rising to its feet, 'I move that the meeting adjourn, for the immediate

adoption of more energetic remedies—'

'Speak English!' said the Eaglet. 'I don't know the meaning of half those long words, and, what's more, I don't believe you do either!' And the Eaglet bent down its head to hide a smile: some of the other birds tittered audibly.

'What I was going to say,' said the Dodo in an offended tone, 'was, that the best thing to get us dry would be a Caucus-race.'

'What *is* a Caucus-race?' said Alice; not that she wanted much to know, but the Dodo had paused as if it thought that *somebody* ought to speak, and no one else seemed inclined to say anything.

'Why,' said the Dodo, 'the best way to explain it is to do it.' (And, as you might like to try the thing yourself, some winter day, I will tell you how the Dodo managed it.)

First it marked out a race-course, in a sort of circle, ('the exact shape doesn't matter,' it said,) and then all the party were placed along the course, here and there. There was no 'One, two, three, and away,' but they began running when they liked, and left off when they liked, so that it was not easy to know when the race was over. However, when they had been running half an hour or so, and were quite dry again, the Dodo suddenly called out 'The race is over!' and they all crowded round it, panting, and asking, 'But who has won?'

This question the Dodo could not answer without a great deal of thought, and it sat for a long time with one finger pressed upon its forehead (the position in which you usually see Shakespeare, in the pictures of him), while the rest waited in silence. At last the Dodo said, '*Everybody* has won, and all must have prizes.'

'But who is to give the prizes?' quite a chorus of voices asked.

'Why, *she*, of course,' said the Dodo, pointing to Alice with one finger; and the whole party at once crowded round her, calling out in a confused way, 'Prizes! Prizes!'

Alice had no idea what to do, and in despair she put her hand in her pocket, and pulled out a box of comfits, (luckily the salt water had not got into it), and handed them round as prizes. There was exactly one a-piece all round.

'But she must have a prize herself, you know,' said the Mouse.

'Of course,' the Dodo replied very gravely. 'What else have you got in your pocket?' he went on, turning to Alice.

'Only a thimble,' said Alice sadly.

'Hand it over here,' said the Dodo.

Then they all crowded round her once more, while the Dodo solemnly presented the thimble, saying 'We beg your acceptance of this elegant thimble'; and, when it had finished this short speech, they all cheered.

Alice thought the whole thing very absurd, but they all looked so grave that she did not dare to laugh; and, as she could not think of anything to say, she simply bowed, and took the thimble, looking as solemn as she could.

The next thing was to eat the comfits: this caused some noise and confusion, as the large birds complained that they could not taste theirs, and the small ones choked and had to be patted on the back. However, it was over at last, and they sat down again in a ring, and begged the Mouse to tell them something more.

'You promised to tell me your history, you know,' said

A CAUCUS-RACE AND A LONG TALE

Alice, 'and why it is you hate—C and D,' she added in a whisper, half afraid that it would be offended again.

'Mine is a long and a sad tale!' said the Mouse, turning to Alice, and sighing.

5 'It *is* a long tail, certainly,' said Alice, looking down with wonder at the Mouse's tail; 'but why do you call it sad?' And she kept on puzzling about it while the Mouse was speaking, so that her idea of the tale was something like this:—

'Fury said to a
mouse, That he
met in the
house,
"Let us
both go to
law: *I* will
prosecute
you. – Come,
I'll take no
denial; We
must have a
trial: For
really this
morning I've
nothing
to do."
Said the
mouse to the
cur, "Such
a trial,
dear Sir,
With
no jury
or judge,
would be
wasting
our
breath."
"I'll be
judge, I'll
be jury,"
Said
cunning
old Fury:
"I'll
try the
whole
cause,
and
condemn
you
to
death."

'You are not attending!' said the Mouse to Alice severely. 'What are you thinking of?'

'I beg your pardon,' said Alice very humbly: 'you had got to the fifth bend, I think?'

'I had *not*!' cried the Mouse, sharply and very angrily.

'A knot!' said Alice, always ready to make herself useful, and looking anxiously about her. 'Oh, do let me help to undo it!'

'I shall do nothing of the sort,' said the Mouse, gettting up and walking away. 'You insult me by talking such nonsense!'

'I didn't mean it!' pleaded poor Alice. 'But you're so easily offended, you know!'

The Mouse only growled in reply.

'Please come back and finish your story!' Alice called after it; and the others all joined in chorus, 'Yes, please do!' but the Mouse only shook its head impatiently, and walked a little quicker.

'What a pity it wouldn't stay!' sighed the Lory, as soon as it was quite out of sight; and an old Crab took the opportunity of saying to her daughter 'Ah, my dear! Let this be a lesson to you never to lose *your* temper!' 'Hold your tongue, Ma!' said the young Crab, a little snappishly. 'You're enough to try the patience of an oyster!'

'I wish I had our Dinah here, I know I do!' said Alice aloud, addressing nobody in particular. 'She'd soon fetch it back!'

'And who is Dinah, if I might venture to ask the question?' said the Lory.

Alice replied eagerly, for she was always ready to talk about her pet: 'Dinah's our cat. And she's such a capital one for catching mice you can't think! And oh, I wish you could see her after the birds! Why, she'll eat a little bird as soon as look at it!'

This speech caused a remarkable sensation among the party. Some of the birds hurried off at once: one old Magpie began wrapping itself up very carefully, remarking, 'I really must be getting home; the night-air doesn't suit my throat!' and a Canary called out in a trembling voice to its children, 'Come away, my dears! It's high time you were all in bed!' On various pretexts they all moved off, and Alice was soon left alone.

'I wish I hadn't mentioned Dinah!' she said to herself in a melancholy tone. 'Nobody seems to like her, down here, and I'm sure she's the best cat in the world! Oh, my dear Dinah! I wonder if I shall ever see you any more!' And here poor Alice began to cry again, for she felt very lonely and low-spirited. In a little while, however, she again heard a little pattering of footsteps in the distance, and she looked up eagerly, half hoping that the Mouse had changed his mind, and was coming back to finish his story.

CHAPTER IV

The Rabbit Sends in a Little Bill

It was the White Rabbit, trotting slowly back again, and looking anxiously about as it went, as if it had lost something; and she heard it muttering to itself 'The Duchess! The Duchess! Oh my dear paws! Oh my fur and whiskers! She'll get me executed, as sure as ferrets are ferrets! Where *can* I have dropped them, I wonder?' Alice guessed in a moment that it was looking for the fan and the pair of white kid gloves, and she very good-naturedly began hunting about for them, but they were nowhere to be seen—everything seemed to have changed since her swim in the pool, and the great hall, with the glass table and the little door, had vanished completely.

Very soon the Rabbit noticed Alice, as she went hunting about, and called out to her in an angry tone, 'Why, Mary Ann, what *are* you doing out here? Run home this moment, and fetch me a pair of gloves and a fan! Quick, now!' And Alice was so much frightened that she ran off at once in the direction it pointed to, without trying to explain the mistake it had made.

'He took me for his housemaid,' she said to herself as she ran. 'How surprised he'll be when he finds out who I am! But I'd better take him his fan and gloves—that is, if I can find them.' As she said this, she came upon a neat little house, on the door of which was a bright brass plate with the name 'W. RABBIT' engraved upon it. She went in without knocking, and hurried upstairs, in great fear lest she should meet the real Mary Ann, and be turned out of the house before she had found the fan and gloves.

'How queer it seems,' Alice said to herself, 'to be going messages for a rabbit! I suppose Dinah'll be sending me on messages next!' And she began fancying the sort of thing that would happen: '"Miss Alice! Come here directly, and get ready for your walk!" "Coming in a minute, nurse! But I've got to watch this mouse-hole till Dinah comes back, and see that the mouse doesn't get out." Only I don't think,' Alice went on, 'that they'd let Dinah stop in the house if it began ordering people about like that!'

By this time she had found her way into a tidy little room with a table in the window, and on it (as she had hoped) a fan and two or three pairs of tiny white kid gloves: she took up the fan and a pair of the gloves, and was just going to leave the room, when her eye fell upon a little bottle that stood near the looking-glass. There was no label this time with the words 'DRINK ME,' but nevertheless she uncorked it and put it to her lips. 'I know *something* interesting is sure to happen,' she said to herself, 'whenever I eat or drink anything; so I'll just see what this bottle does. I do hope it'll make me grow large again, for really I'm quite tired of being such a tiny little thing!'

THE RABBIT SENDS IN A LITTLE BILL

It did so indeed, and much sooner than she had expected: before she had drunk half the bottle, she found her head pressing against the ceiling, and had to stoop to save her neck from being broken. She hastily put down the bottle, saying to herself 'That's quite enough—I hope I shan't grow any more—As it is, I can't get out at the door—I do wish I hadn't drunk quite so much!'

Alas! it was too late to wish that! She went on growing, and growing, and very soon had to kneel down on the floor: in another minute there was not even room for this, and she tried the effect of lying down with one elbow against the door, and the other arm curled round her head. Still she went on growing, and, as a last resource, she put one arm out of the window, and one foot up the chimney, and said to herself 'Now I can do no more, whatever happens. What *will* become of me?'

Luckily for Alice, the little magic bottle had now had its full effect, and she grew no larger: still it was very uncomfortable, and, as there seemed to be no sort of chance of her ever getting out of the room again, no wonder she felt unhappy.

'It was much pleasanter at home,' thought poor Alice, 'when one wasn't always growing larger and smaller, and being ordered about by mice and rabbits. I almost wish I hadn't gone down that rabbit-hole—and yet—and yet—it's rather curious, you know, this sort of life! I do wonder what *can* have happened to me! When I used to read fairy-tales, I fancied that kind of thing never happened, and now here I am in the middle of one! There ought to be a book written about me, that there ought! And when I grow up, I'll write one—but I'm grown up now,' she added in a sorrowful tone; 'at least there's no room to grow up any more *here*.'

'But then,' thought Alice, 'shall I *never* get any older than I am now? That'll be a comfort, one way—never to be an old woman—but then—always to have lessons to learn! Oh, I shouldn't like *that*!'

'Oh, you foolish Alice!' she answered herself. 'How can you learn lessons in here? Why, there's hardly room for *you*, and no room at all for any lesson-books!'

And so she went on, talking first one side and then the other, and making quite a conversation of it altogether; but after a few minutes she heard a voice outside, and stopped to listen.

'Mary Ann! Mary Ann!' said the voice. 'Fetch me my gloves this moment!' Then came a little pattering

THE RABBIT SENDS IN A LITTLE BILL

of feet on the stairs. Alice knew it was the Rabbit coming to look for her, and she trembled till she shook the house, quite forgetting that she was now about a thousand times as large as the Rabbit, and had no reason
5 to be afraid of it.

Presently the Rabbit came up to the door, and tried to open it; but, as the door opened inwards, and Alice's elbow was pressed hard against it, that attempt proved a failure. Alice heard it say to itself ' Then I'll go round
10 and get in at the window.'

' *That* you won't!' thought Alice, and, after waiting till she fancied she heard the Rabbit just under the window, she suddenly spread out her hand, and made a snatch in the air. She did not get hold of anything, but she heard
15 a little shriek and a fall, and a crash of broken glass, from which she concluded that it was just possible it had fallen into a cucumber-frame, or something of the sort.

Next came an angry voice— the Rabbit's—' Pat! Pat! Where
20 are you?' And then a voice she had never heard before, ' Sure then I'm here! Digging for apples, yer honour!'

' Digging for apples, indeed!'
25 said the Rabbit angrily. ' Here! Come and help me out of *this*!' (Sounds of more broken glass.)

' Now tell me, Pat, what's that

in the window?'

'Sure, it's an arm, yer honour!' (He pronounced it 'arrum.')

'An arm, you goose! Who ever saw one that size? Why, it fills the whole window!'

'Sure, it does, yer honour: but it's an arm for all that.'

'Well, it's got no business there, at any rate: go and take it away!'

There was a long silence after this, and Alice could only hear whispers now and then; such as, 'Sure, I don't like it, yer honour, at all, at all!' 'Do as I tell you, you coward!' and at last she spread out her hand again, and made another snatch in the air. This time there were *two* little shrieks, and more sounds of broken glass. 'What a number of cucumber-frames there must be!' thought Alice. 'I wonder what they'll do next! As for pulling me out of the window, I only wish they *could*! I'm sure *I* don't want to stay in here any longer!'

She waited for some time without hearing anything more: at last came a rumbling of little cart-wheels, and the sound of a good many voices all talking together: she made out the words: 'Where's the other ladder?— Why, I hadn't to bring but one; Bill's got the other— Bill! fetch it here, lad!—Here, put 'em up at this corner —No, tie 'em together first—they don't reach half high enough yet—Oh! they'll do well enough; don't be particular—Here, Bill! catch hold of this rope—Will the roof bear?—Mind that loose slate—Oh, it's coming down!

Heads below!' (a loud crash)—'Now, who did that?—It was Bill, I fancy—Who's to go down the chimney?—Nay, *I* shan't! *You* do it!—*That* I won't, then!—Bill's got to go down—Here, Bill! the master says you've got to go down the chimney!'

'Oh! So Bill's got to come down the chimney, has he?' said Alice to herself. 'Why, they seem to put everything upon Bill! I wouldn't be in Bill's place for a good deal: this fire-place is narrow, to be sure; but I *think* I can kick a little!'

She drew her foot as far down the chimney as she could, and waited till she heard a little animal (she couldn't guess of what sort it was) scratching and scrambling about in the chimney close above her: then, saying to herself 'This is Bill,' she gave one sharp kick, and waited to see what would happen next.

The first thing she heard was a general chorus of 'There goes Bill!' then the Rabbit's voice alone—'Catch him, you by the hedge!' then silence, and then another confusion of voices—'Hold up his head—Brandy now—Don't choke him —How was it, old fellow? What happened to you? Tell us all about it!'

Last came a little feeble, squeaking voice, ('That's Bill,' thought Alice,) 'Well, I hardly know — No more, thank ye; I'm better now — but I'm a deal too flustered to tell you — all I know is, something comes at me like a Jack-in-the-box, and up I goes like a sky-rocket!'

'So you did, old fellow!' said the others.

'We must burn the house down!' said the Rabbit's voice; and Alice called out as loud as she could, 'If you do, I'll set Dinah at you!'

There was a dead silence instantly, and Alice thought to herself, 'I wonder what they *will* do next! If they had any sense, they'd take the roof off.' After a minute or two, they began moving about again, and Alice heard the Rabbit say, 'A barrowful will do, to begin with.'

'A barrowful of *what*?' thought Alice; but she had not long to doubt, for the next moment a shower of little pebbles came rattling in at the window, and some of them hit her in the face. 'I'll put a stop to this,' she said to herself, and shouted out, 'You'd better not do that again!' which produced another dead silence.

Alice noticed with some surprise that the pebbles were all turning into little cakes as they lay on the floor, and a bright idea came into her head. 'If I eat one of these cakes,' she thought, 'it's sure to make *some* change in my size; and as it can't possibly make me larger, it must make me smaller, I suppose.'

So she swallowed one of the cakes, and was delighted

THE RABBIT SENDS IN A LITTLE BILL

to find that she began shrinking directly. As soon as she was small enough to get through the door, she ran out of the house, and found quite a crowd of little animals and birds waiting outside. The poor little Lizard, Bill, was in the middle, being held up by two guinea-pigs, who were giving it something out of a bottle. They all made a rush at Alice the moment she appeared; but she ran off as hard as she could, and soon found herself safe in a thick wood.

'The first thing I've got to do,' said Alice to herself, as she wandered about in the wood, 'is to grow to my right size again; and the second thing is to find my way into that lovely garden. I think that will be the best plan.'

It sounded an excellent plan, no doubt, and very neatly and simply arranged; the only difficulty was, that she had not the smallest idea how to set about it; and while she was peering about anxiously among the trees, a little sharp bark just over her head made her look up in a great hurry.

An enormous puppy was looking down at her with large round eyes, and feebly stretching out one paw, trying to touch her. 'Poor little thing!' said Alice, in a coaxing tone, and she tried hard to whistle to it; but she was terribly frightened all the time at the thought that it might be hungry, in which case it would be very likely to eat her up in spite of all her coaxing.

Hardly knowing what she did, she picked up a little

bit of stick, and held it out to the puppy; whereupon the puppy jumped into the air off all its feet at once, with a yelp of delight, and rushed at the stick, and made believe to worry it; then Alice dodged behind a great thistle, to keep herself from being run over; and the moment she appeared on the other side, the puppy made another rush at the stick, and tumbled head over heels in its hurry to get hold of it; then Alice, thinking it was very like having a game of play with a cart-horse, and expecting every moment to be trampled under its feet, ran round the thistle again; then the puppy began a series of short charges at the stick, running a very little way forwards each time and a long way back, and barking hoarsely all the while, till at last it sat down a good way off, panting, with its tongue hanging out of its mouth, and its great eyes half shut.

5 This seemed to Alice a good opportunity for making her escape; so she set off at once, and ran till she was quite tired and out of breath, and till the puppy's bark sounded quite faint in the distance.

'And yet what a dear little puppy it was!' said Alice,
10 as she leant against a buttercup to rest herself, and fanned herself with one of the leaves: 'I should have liked teaching it tricks very much, if — if I'd only been the right size to do it! Oh dear! I'd nearly forgotten that I've got to grow up again! Let me see — how *is* it
15 to be managed? I suppose I ought to eat or drink something or other; but the great question is, what?'

The great question certainly was, what? Alice looked all round her at the flowers and the blades of grass, but she could not see anything that looked like the right
20 thing to eat or drink under the circumstances. There was a large mushroom growing near her, about the same height as herself; and when she had looked under it, and on both sides of it, and behind it, it occurred to her that she might as well look and see what was on the
25 top of it.

She stretched herself up on tiptoe, and peeped over the edge of the mushroom, and her eyes immediately met those of a large blue caterpillar, that was sitting on the top with its arms folded, quietly smoking a long hookah, and taking not the smallest notice of her or of anything else.

CHAPTER V

Advice from a Caterpillar

The Caterpillar and Alice looked at each other for some time in silence: at last the Caterpillar took the hookah out of its mouth, and addressed her in a languid, sleepy voice.

5 'Who are *you*?' said the Caterpillar.

This was not an encouraging opening for a conversation. Alice replied, rather shyly, 'I-I hardly know, sir, just at present — at least I know who I *was* when I got up this morning, but I think I must have been changed several times since then.'

'What do you mean by that?' said the Caterpillar sternly. 'Explain yourself!'

'I can't explain *myself*, I'm afraid, sir,' said Alice, 'because I'm not myself, you see.'

'I don't see,' said the Caterpillar.

'I'm afraid I can't put it more clearly,' Alice replied very politely, 'for I can't understand it myself to begin with; and being so many different sizes in a day is very confusing.'

'It isn't,' said the Caterpillar.

'Well, perhaps you haven't found it so yet,' said Alice; 'but when you have to turn into a chrysalis—you will some day, you know—and then after that into a butterfly, I should think you'll feel it a little queer, won't you?'

'Not a bit,' said the Caterpillar.

'Well, perhaps *your* feelings may be different,' said Alice; 'all I know is, it would feel very queer to *me*.'

'You!' said the Caterpillar contemptuously. 'Who are *you*?'

Which brought them back again to the beginning of the conversation. Alice felt a little irritated at the Caterpillar's making such *very* short remarks, and she drew herself up and said, very gravely, 'I think you ought to tell me who *you* are, first.'

'Why?' said the Caterpillar.

Here was another puzzling question; and as Alice

ADVICE FROM A CATERPILLAR

could not think of any good reason, and as the Caterpillar seemed to be in a *very* unpleasant state of mind, she turned away.

'Come back!' the Caterpillar called after her. 'I've
5 something important to say!'

This sounded promising, certainly: Alice turned and came back again.

'Keep your temper,' said the Caterpillar.

'Is that all?' said Alice, swallowing down her anger
10 as well as she could.

'No,' said the Caterpillar.

Alice thought she might as well wait, as she had nothing else to do, and perhaps after all it might tell her something worth hearing. For some minutes it puffed
15 away without speaking, but at last it unfolded its arms, took the hookah out of its mouth again, and said, 'So you think you're changed, do you?'

'I'm afraid I am, Sir,' said Alice; 'I can't remember things as I used—and I don't keep the same size for ten
20 minutes together!'

'Can't remember *what* things?' said the Caterpillar.

'Well, I've tried to say "*How doth the little busy bee,*" but it all came different!' Alice replied in a very melancholy voice.

25 'Repeat, "*You are old, Father William,*"' said the Caterpillar.

Alice folded her hands, and began:—

'You are old, Father William,' the young man said,
  'And your hair has become very white;
And yet you incessantly stand on your head—
  Do you think, at your age, it is right?'

'In my youth,' Father William replied to his son, 5
  'I feared it might injure the brain;
But, now that I'm perfectly sure I have none,
  Why, I do it again and again.'

'You are old,' said the youth, 'as I mentioned before,
  And have grown most uncommonly fat; 10
Yet you turned a back-somersault in at the door—
  Pray, what is the reason of that?'

'In my youth,' said the sage, as he shook his grey locks,
  'I kept all my limbs very supple
By the use of this ointment—one shilling the box— 15
  Allow me to sell you a couple?'

ADVICE FROM A CATERPILLAR

'You are old,' said the youth, 'and your jaws are too weak
    For anything tougher than suet;
Yet you finished the goose, with the bones and the beak —
    Pray how did you manage to do it?'

'In my youth,' said his father, 'I took to the law,
    And argued each case with my wife;
And the muscular strength, which it gave to my jaw,
    Has lasted the rest of my life.'

'You are old,' said the youth, 'one would hardly suppose
    That your eye was as steady as ever;
Yet you balanced an eel on the end of your nose —
    What made you so awfully clever?'

'I have answered three questions, and that is enough,'
    Said his father; 'don't give yourself airs!
Do you think I can listen all day to such stuff?
    Be off, or I'll kick you down stairs!'

'That is not said right,' said the Caterpillar.

'Not *quite* right, I'm afraid,' said Alice, timidly; 'some of the words have got altered.'

'It is wrong from beginning to end,' said the Caterpillar decidedly, and there was silence for some minutes.

The Caterpillar was the first to speak.

'What size do you want to be?' it asked.

'Oh, I'm not particular as to size,' Alice hastily replied; 'only one doesn't like changing so often, you know.'

'I *don't* know,' said the Caterpillar.

Alice said nothing: she had never been so much contradicted in all her life before, and she felt that she was losing her temper.

'Are you content now?' said the Caterpillar.

'Well, I should like to be a *little* larger, sir, if you wouldn't mind,' said Alice: 'three inches is such a

ADVICE FROM A CATERPILLAR

wretched height to be.'

'It is a very good height indeed!' said the Caterpillar angrily, rearing itself upright as it spoke (it was exactly three inches high).

5 'But I'm not used to it!' pleaded poor Alice in a piteous tone. And she thought to herself, 'I wish the creatures wouldn't be so easily offended!'

'You'll get used to it in time,' said the Caterpillar; and it put the hookah into its mouth and began smoking 10 again.

This time Alice waited patiently until it chose to speak again. In a minute or two the Caterpillar took the hookah out of its mouth and yawned once or twice, and shook itself. Then it got down off the mushroom, and 15 crawled away into the grass, merely remarking as it went, 'One side will make you grow taller, and the other side will make you grow shorter.'

'One side of *what*? The other side of *what*?' thought Alice to herself.

'Of the mushroom,' said the Caterpillar, just as if she had asked it aloud; and in another moment it was out of sight.

Alice remained looking thoughtfully at the mushroom for a minute, trying to make out which were the two sides of it; and as it was perfectly round, she found this a very difficult question. However, at last she stretched her arms round it as far as they would go, and broke off a bit of the edge with each hand.

'And now which is which?' she said to herself, and nibbled a little of the right-hand bit to try the effect. The next moment she felt a violent blow underneath her chin: it had struck her foot!

She was a good deal frightened by this very sudden change, but she felt that there was no time to be lost, as she was shrinking rapidly; so she set to work at once to eat some of the other bit. Her chin was pressed so closely against her foot, that there was hardly room to open her mouth; but she did it at last, and managed to swallow a morsel of the left-hand bit.

   * * * * *

'Come, my head's free at last!' said Alice in a tone of delight, which changed into alarm in another moment, when she found that her shoulders were nowhere to be found: all she could see, when she looked down, was an

ADVICE FROM A CATERPILLAR

immense length of neck, which seemed to rise like a stalk out of a sea of green leaves that lay far below her.

'What *can* all that green stuff be?' said Alice. 'And where *have* my shoulders got to? And oh, my poor hands, how is it I can't see you?' She was moving them about as she spoke, but no result seemed to follow, except a little shaking among the distant green leaves.

As there seemed to be no chance of getting her hands up to her head, she tried to get her head down to them, and was delighted to find that her neck would bend about easily in any direction, like a serpent. She had just succeeded in curving it down into a graceful zigzag, and was going to dive in among the leaves, which she found to be nothing but the tops of the trees under which she had been wandering, when a sharp hiss made her draw back in a hurry: a large pigeon had flown into her face, and was beating her violently with its wings.

'Serpent!' screamed the Pigeon.

'I'm *not* a serpent!' said Alice indignantly. 'Let me alone!'

'Serpent, I say again!' repeated the Pigeon, but in a more subdued tone, and added with a kind of sob, 'I've tried every way, and nothing seems to suit them!'

'I haven't the least idea what you're talking about,' said Alice.

'I've tried the roots of trees, and I've tried banks, and I've tried hedges,' the Pigeon went on, without attending to her; 'but those serpents! There's no pleasing them!'

Alice was more and more puzzled, but she thought there was no use in saying anything more till the Pigeon had finished.

'As if it wasn't trouble enough hatching the eggs,' said the Pigeon; 'but I must be on the look-out for serpents night and day! Why, I haven't had a wink of sleep these three weeks!'

'I'm very sorry you've been annoyed,' said Alice, who was beginning to see its meaning.

'And just as I'd taken the highest tree in the wood,' continued the Pigeon, raising its voice to a shriek, 'and just as I was thinking I should be free of them at last, they must needs come wriggling down from the sky! Ugh, Serpent!'

'But I'm *not* a serpent, I tell you!' said Alice. 'I'm a —I'm a—'

'Well! *What* are you?' said the Pigeon. 'I can see you're trying to invent something!'

'I—I'm a little girl,' said Alice, rather doubtfully, as she remembered the number of changes she had gone through that day.

'A likely story indeed!' said the Pigeon in a tone of the deepest contempt. 'I've seen a good many little girls in my time, but never *one* with such a neck as that! No, no! You're a serpent; and there's no use denying it. I suppose you'll be telling me next that you never tasted an egg!'

'I *have* tasted eggs, certainly,' said Alice, who was a

very truthful child; 'but little girls eat eggs quite as much as serpents do, you know.'

'I don't believe it,' said the Pigeon; 'but if they do, why then they're a kind of serpent, that's all I can say.'

This was such a new idea to Alice, that she was quite silent for a minute or two, which gave the Pigeon the opportunity of adding, ' You're looking for eggs, I know *that* well enough; and what does it matter to me whether you're a little girl or a serpent?'

'It matters a good deal to *me*,' said Alice hastily; 'but I'm not looking for eggs, as it happens; and if I was, I shouldn't want *yours*: I don't like them raw.'

'Well, be off, then!' said the Pigeon in a sulky tone, as it settled down again into its nest. Alice crouched down among the trees as well as she could, for her neck kept getting entangled among the branches, and every now and then she had to stop and untwist it. After a while she remembered that she still held the pieces of mushroom in her hands, and she set to work very carefully, nibbling first at one and then at the other, and growing sometimes taller and sometimes shorter, until she had succeeded in bringing herself down to her usual height.

It was so long since she had been anything near the right size, that it felt quite strange at first; but she got used to it in a few minutes, and began talking to herself, as usual. 'Come, there's half my plan done now! How puzzling all these changes are! I'm never sure what I'm going to be, from one minute to another! However, I've got back to my right size: the next thing is, to get into that beautiful garden—how *is* that to be done, I wonder?' As she said this, she came suddenly upon an open place, with a little house in it about four feet high. 'Whoever lives there,' thought Alice, 'it'll never do to come upon them *this* size: why, I should frighten them out of their wits!' So she began nibbling at the right-hand bit again, and did not venture to go near the house till she had brought herself down to nine inches high.

CHAPTER VI

Pig and Pepper

For a minute or two she stood looking at the house, and wondering what to do next, when suddenly a footman in livery came running out of the wood—(she considered him to be a footman because he was in livery: otherwise, judging by his face only, she would have called him a fish)—and rapped loudly at the door with his knuckles. It was opened by another footman in livery, with a round face, and large eyes like a frog; and both footmen, Alice noticed, had powdered hair that curled all over their heads. She felt very curious to know what it was all about, and crept a little way out of the wood to listen.

The Fish-Footman began by producing from under his arm a great letter, nearly as large as himself, and this he handed over to the other, saying, in a solemn tone, 'For the Duchess. An invitation from the Queen to play croquet.' The Frog-Footman repeated, in the same solemn tone, only changing the order of the words a little, 'From the Queen. An invitation for the Duchess to play croquet.'

Then they both bowed low, and their curls got entangled together.

Alice laughed so much at this, that she had to run back into the wood for fear of their hearing her; and when she next peeped out the Fish-Footman was gone, and the other was sitting on the ground near the door, staring stupidly up into the sky.

Alice went timidly up to the door, and knocked.

'There's no sort of use in knocking,' said the Footman, 'and that for two reasons. First, because I'm on the same side of the door as you are; secondly, because they're making such a noise inside, no one could possibly hear you.' And certainly there was a most extraordinary noise going on within—a constant howling and sneezing, and every now and then a great crash, as if a dish or kettle had been broken to pieces.

'Please, then,' said Alice, 'how am I to get in?'

'There might be some sense in your knocking,' the Footman went on without attending to her, 'if we had the door between us. For instance, if you were *inside*, you might knock, and I could let you out, you know.' He was looking up into the sky all the time he was speaking, and this Alice thought decidedly uncivil. 'But perhaps he can't help it,' she said to herself; 'his eyes are so *very* nearly at the top of his head. But at any rate he might answer questions.— How am I to get in?' she repeated, aloud.

'I shall sit here,' the Footman remarked, 'till tomorrow —'

At this moment the door of the house opened, and a large plate came skimming out, straight at the Footman's head: it just grazed his nose, and broke to pieces against one of the trees behind him.

'— or next day, maybe,' the Footman continued in the same tone, exactly as if nothing had happened.

'How am I to get in?' asked Alice again, in a louder tone.

'*Are* you to get in at all?' said the Footman. 'That's the first question, you know.'

It was, no doubt: only Alice did not like to be told so. 'It's really dreadful,' she muttered to herself, 'the way all the creatures argue. It's enough to drive one crazy!'

The Footman seemed to think this a good opportunity for repeating his remark, with variations. 'I shall sit here,' he said, 'on and off, for days and days.'

'But what am *I* to do?' said Alice.

'Anything you like,' said the Footman, and began whistling.

'Oh, there's no use in talking to him,' said Alice desperately: 'he's perfectly idiotic!' And she opened the door and went in.

The door led right into a large kitchen, which was full of smoke from one end to the other: the Duchess was sitting on a three-legged stool in the middle, nursing a baby; the cook was leaning over the fire, stirring a large cauldron which seemed to be full of soup.

'There's certainly too much pepper in that soup!' Alice said to herself, as well as she could for sneezing.

There was certainly too much of it in the air. Even the Duchess sneezed occasionally; and as for the baby, it was sneezing and howling alternately without a moment's pause. The only things in the kitchen that did

PIG AND PEPPER

not sneeze, were the cook, and a large cat which was sitting on the hearth and grinning from ear to ear.

'Please would you tell me,' said Alice, a little timidly, for she was not quite sure whether it was good manners for her to speak first, 'why your cat grins like that?'

'It's a Cheshire cat,' said the Duchess, 'and that's why. Pig!'

She said the last word with such sudden violence that Alice quite jumped; but she saw in another moment that it was addressed to the baby, and not to her, so she took courage, and went on again:—

'I didn't know that Cheshire cats always grinned; in fact, I didn't know that cats *could* grin.'

'They all can,' said the Duchess; 'and most of 'em do.'

'I don't know of any that do,' Alice said very politely, feeling quite pleased to have got into a conversation.

'You don't know much,' said the Duchess; 'and that's a fact.'

Alice did not at all like the tone of this remark, and thought it would be as well to introduce some other subject of conversation. While she was trying to fix on one, the cook took the cauldron of soup off the fire, and at once set to work throwing everything within her reach at the Duchess and the baby — the fire-irons came first; then followed a shower of saucepans, plates, and dishes. The Duchess took no notice of them even when they hit her; and the baby was howling so much already, that it was quite impossible to say whether the blows hurt it or not.

'Oh, *please* mind what you're doing!' cried Alice, jumping up and down in an agony of terror. 'Oh, there goes his *precious* nose'; as an unusually large saucepan flew close by it, and very nearly carried it off.

'If everybody minded their own business,' the Duchess said in a hoarse growl, 'the world would go round a deal faster than it does.'

'Which would *not* be an advantage,' said Alice, who felt very glad to get an opportunity of showing off a little of her knowledge. 'Just think of what work it would make with the day and night! You see the earth takes twenty-four hours to turn round on its axis — '

'Talking of axes,' said the Duchess, 'chop off her head!'

Alice glanced rather anxiously at the cook, to see if she meant to take the hint; but the cook was busily stirring the soup, and seemed not to be listening, so she went on again: 'Twenty-four hours, I *think*; or is it twelve? I — '

'Oh, don't bother *me*,' said the Duchess; 'I never could abide figures!' And with that she began nursing her child again, singing a sort of lullaby to it as she did so, and giving it a violent shake at the end of every line:

> '*Speak roughly to your little boy,*
> *And beat him when he sneezes:*
> *He only does it to annoy,*
> *Because he knows it teases.*'

CHORUS.

(In which the cook and the baby joined): —
'*Wow! wow! wow!*'

While the Duchess sang the second verse of the song, she kept tossing the baby violently up and down, and the poor little thing howled so, that Alice could hardly hear the words: —

> '*I speak severely to my boy,*
> *I beat him when he sneezes;*
> *For he can thoroughly enjoy*
> *The pepper when he pleases!*'

CHORUS.
'*Wow! wow! wow!*'

'Here! you may nurse it a bit, if you like!' the Duchess said to Alice, flinging the baby at her as she spoke. 'I must go and get ready to play croquet with the Queen,' and she hurried out of the room. The cook threw a frying-pan after her as she went out, but it just missed her.

Alice caught the baby with some difficulty, as it was a queer-shaped little creature, and held out its arms and legs in all directions, 'just like a star-fish,' thought Alice. The poor little thing was snorting like a steam-engine when she caught it, and kept doubling itself up and straightening itself out again, so that altogether, for the first minute or two, it was as much as she could do to hold it.

As soon as she had made out the proper way of nursing it, (which was to twist it up into a sort of knot, and then keep tight hold of its right ear and left foot, so as to prevent its undoing itself,) she carried it out into the open air. 'If I don't take this child away with me,' thought Alice, 'they're sure to kill it in a day or two: wouldn't it be murder to leave it behind?' She said the last words out loud, and the little thing grunted in reply (it had left off sneezing by this time). 'Don't grunt,' said Alice; 'that's not at all a proper way of expressing yourself.'

The baby grunted again, and Alice looked very anxiously into its face to see what was the matter with it. There could be no doubt that it had a *very* turn-up nose, much more like a snout than a real nose; also its eyes were getting extremely small for a baby: altogether Alice did not like the look of the thing at all. 'But perhaps it was only sobbing,' she thought, and looked into its eyes again, to see if there were any tears.

No, there were no tears. 'If you're going to turn into a pig, my dear,' said Alice, seriously, 'I'll have nothing more to do with you. Mind now!' The

PIG AND PEPPER

poor little thing sobbed again (or grunted, it was impossible to say which), and they went on for some while in silence.

Alice was just beginning to think to herself, 'Now, what am I to do with this creature when I get it home?' when it grunted again, so violently, that she looked down into its face in some alarm. This time there could be *no* mistake about it: it was neither more nor less than a pig, and she felt that it would be quite absurd for her to carry it any further.

So she set the little creature down, and felt quite relieved to see it trot away quietly into the wood. 'If it had grown up,' she said to herself, 'it would have made a dreadfully ugly child: but it makes rather a handsome pig, I think.' And she began thinking over other children she knew, who might do very well as pigs, and was just saying to herself, 'if one only knew the right way to change them —' when she was a little startled by seeing the Cheshire Cat sitting on a bough of a tree a few yards off.

The Cat only grinned when it saw Alice. It looked good-natured, she thought: still it had *very* long claws and a great many teeth, so she felt that it ought to be treated with respect.

'Cheshire Puss,' she began, rather timidly, as she did not at all know whether it would like the name: however, it only grinned a little wider. 'Come, it's pleased so far,' thought Alice, and she went on. 'Would you tell me, please, which way I ought to go from here?'

'That depends a good deal on where you want to get to,' said the Cat.

'I don't much care where —' said Alice.

'Then it doesn't matter which way you go,' said the Cat.

'—so long as I get *somewhere*,' Alice added as an explanation.

'Oh, you're sure to do that,' said the Cat, 'if you only walk long enough.'

Alice felt that this could not be denied, so she tried another question. 'What sort of people live about here?'

'In *that* direction,' the Cat said, waving its right paw round, 'lives a Hatter: and in *that* direction,' waving the other paw, 'lives a March Hare. Visit either you like: they're both mad.'

'But I don't want to go among mad people,' Alice remarked.

'Oh, you can't help that,' said the Cat: 'we're all mad here. I'm mad. You're mad.'

'How do you know I'm mad?' said Alice.

'You must be,' said the Cat, 'or you wouldn't have come here.'

Alice didn't think that proved it at all; however, she went on 'And how do you know that you're mad?'

'To begin with,' said the Cat, 'a dog's not mad. You grant that?'

'I suppose so,' said Alice.

'Well, then,' the Cat went on, 'you see, a dog growls

PIG AND PEPPER 63

when it's angry, and wags its tail when it's pleased. Now *I* growl when I'm pleased, and wag my tail when I'm angry. Therefore I'm mad.'

'*I* call it purring, not growling,' said Alice.

'Call it what you like,' said the Cat. 'Do you play croquet with the Queen to-day?'

'I should like it very much,' said Alice, 'but I haven't been invited yet.'

'You'll see me there,' said the Cat, and vanished.

Alice was not much surprised at this, she was getting so used to queer things happening. While she was looking at the place where it had been, it suddenly appeared again.

'By-the-bye, what became of the baby?' said the Cat. 'I'd nearly forgotten to ask.'

'It turned into a pig,' Alice quietly said, just as if it had come back in a natural way.

'I thought it would,' said the Cat, and vanished again.

Alice waited a little, half expecting to see it again, but it did not appear, and after a minute or two she walked on in the direction in which the March Hare was said to live. 'I've seen hatters before,' she said to herself; 'the March Hare will be much the most interesting, and perhaps as this is May it won't be raving mad—at least not so mad as it was in March.' As she said this, she looked up, and there was the Cat again, sitting on a branch of a tree.

'Did you say pig, or fig?' said the Cat.

'I said pig,' replied Alice; 'and I wish you wouldn't keep appearing and vanishing so suddenly: you make one quite giddy.'

'All right,' said the Cat; and this time it vanished quite slowly, beginning with the end of the tail, and ending with the grin, which remained some time after the rest of it had gone.

'Well! I've often seen a cat without a grin,' thought Alice; 'but a grin without a cat! It's the most curious thing I ever saw in all my life!'

She had not gone much farther before she came in sight of the house of the March Hare: she thought it must be the right house, because the chimneys were shaped like ears and the roof was thatched with fur. It was so large a house, that she did not like to go nearer till she had nibbled some more of the left-hand bit of mushroom, and raised herself to about two feet high: even then she walked up towards it rather timidly, say-

ing to herself 'Suppose it should be raving mad after all! I almost wish I'd gone to see the Hatter instead!'

CHAPTER VII

A Mad Tea-Party

There was a table set out under a tree in front of the house, and the March Hare and the Hatter were having tea at it: a Dormouse was sitting between them, fast asleep, and the other two were using it as a cushion, resting their elbows on it, and talking over its head. 'Very uncomfortable for the Dormouse,' thought Alice; 'only, as it's asleep, I suppose it doesn't mind.'

The table was a large one, but the three were all crowded together at one corner of it: 'No room! No room!' they cried out when they saw Alice coming. 'There's *plenty* of room!' said Alice indignantly, and she sat down in a large arm-chair at one end of the table.

'Have some wine,' the March Hare said in an encouraging tone.

Alice looked all round the table, but there was nothing on it but tea. 'I don't see any wine,' she remarked.

'There isn't any,' said the March Hare.

'Then it wasn't very civil of you to offer it,' said Alice angrily.

'It wasn't very civil of you to sit down without being invited,' said the March Hare.

'I didn't know it was *your* table,' said Alice; 'it's laid for a great many more than three.'

'Your hair wants cutting,' said the Hatter. He had

been looking at Alice for some time with great curiosity, and this was his first speech.

'You should learn not to make personal remarks,' Alice said with some severity; 'it's very rude.'

5 The Hatter opened his eyes very wide on hearing this; but all he *said* was, 'Why is a raven like a writing-desk?'

'Come, we shall have some fun now!' thought Alice. 'I'm glad they've begun asking riddles.—I believe I can
10 guess that,' she added aloud.

'Do you mean that you think you can find out the answer to it?' said the March Hare.

'Exactly so,' said Alice.

'Then you should say what you mean,' the March
15 Hare went on.

'I do,' Alice hastily replied; 'at least—at least I mean what I say—that's the same thing, you know.'

'Not the same thing a bit!' said the Hatter. 'You might just as well say that "I see what I eat" is the same thing as "I eat what I see"!'

'You might just as well say,' added the March Hare, 'that "I like what I get" is the same thing as "I get what I like"!'

'You might just as well say,' added the Dormouse, who seemed to be talking in his sleep, 'that "I breathe when I sleep" is the same thing as "I sleep when I breathe"!'

'It *is* the same thing with you,' said the Hatter, and here the conversation dropped, and the party sat silent for a minute, while Alice thought over all she could remember about ravens and writing-desks, which wasn't much.

The Hatter was the first to break the silence. 'What day of the month is it?' he said, turning to Alice: he had taken his watch out of his pocket, and was looking at it uneasily, shaking it every now and then, and holding it to his ear.

Alice considered a little, and then said 'The fourth.'

'Two days wrong!' sighed the Hatter. 'I told you butter wouldn't suit the works!' he added, looking angrily at the March Hare.

'It was the *best* butter,' the March Hare meekly replied.

'Yes, but some crumbs must have got in as well,' the Hatter grumbled: 'you shouldn't have put it in with the bread-knife.'

The March Hare took the watch and looked at it

gloomily: then he dipped it into his cup of tea, and looked at it again: but he could think of nothing better to say than his first remark, 'It was the *best* butter, you know.'

Alice had been looking over his shoulder with some curiosity. 'What a funny watch!' she remarked. 'It tells the day of the month, and doesn't tell what o'clock it is!'

'Why should it?' muttered the Hatter. 'Does *your* watch tell you what year it is?'

'Of course not,' Alice replied very readily: 'but that's because it stays the same year for such a long time together.'

'Which is just the case with *mine*,' said the Hatter.

Alice felt dreadfully puzzled. The Hatter's remark seemed to have no sort of meaning in it, and yet it was certainly English. 'I don't quite understand you,' she said, as politely as she could.

'The Dormouse is asleep again,' said the Hatter, and he poured a little hot tea upon its nose.

The Dormouse shook its head impatiently, and said, without opening its eyes, 'Of course, of course; just what I was going to remark myself.'

'Have you guessed the riddle yet?' the Hatter said, turning to Alice again.

'No, I give it up,' Alice replied: 'what's the answer?'

'I haven't the slightest idea,' said the Hatter.

'Nor I,' said the March Hare.

Alice sighed wearily. 'I think you might do something better with the time,' she said, 'than waste it in asking riddles that have no answers.'

'If you knew Time as well as I do,' said the Hatter, 'you wouldn't talk about wasting *it*. It's *him*.'

'I don't know what you mean,' said Alice.

'Of course you don't!' the Hatter said, tossing his head contemptuously. 'I dare say you never even spoke to Time!'

'Perhaps not,' Alice cautiously replied: 'but I know I have to beat time when I learn music.'

'Ah! that accounts for it,' said the Hatter. 'He won't stand beating. Now, if you only kept on good terms with him, he'd do almost anything you liked with the clock. For instance, suppose it were nine o'clock in the morning, just time to begin lessons: you'd only have to whisper a hint to Time, and round goes the clock in a twinkling! Half-past one, time for dinner!'

('I only wish it was,' the March Hare said to itself in a whisper.)

'That would be grand, certainly,' said Alice thoughtfully: 'but then—I shouldn't be hungry for it, you know.'

'Not at first, perhaps,' said the Hatter: 'but you could keep it to half-past one as long as you liked.'

'Is that the way *you* manage?' Alice asked.

The Hatter shook his head mournfully. 'Not I!' he replied. 'We quarrelled last March—just before *he* went mad, you know—' (pointing with his tea-spoon at the March Hare,) '— it was at the great concert given by the Queen of Hearts, and I had to sing

> "*Twinkle, twinkle, little bat!*
> *How I wonder what you're at!*"

You know the song, perhaps?'

'I've heard something like it,' said Alice.

'It goes on, you know,' the Hatter continued, 'in this way:—

> "*Up above the world you fly,*
> *Like a tea-tray in the sky.*
> *Twinkle, twinkle —*"'

Here the Dormouse shook itself, and began singing in its sleep '*Twinkle, twinkle, twinkle, twinkle —*' and went on so long that they had to pinch it to make it stop.

'Well, I'd hardly finished the first verse,' said the Hatter, 'when the Queen jumped up and bawled out, "He's murdering the time! Off with his head!"'

'How dreadfully savage!' exclaimed Alice.

'And ever since that,' the Hatter went on in a mournful tone, 'he won't do a thing I ask! It's always six o'clock now.'

A bright idea came into Alice's head. 'Is that the reason so many tea-things are put out here?' she asked.

'Yes, that's it,' said the Hatter with a sigh: 'it's

always tea-time, and we've no time to wash the things between whiles.'

'Then you keep moving round, I suppose?' said Alice.

'Exactly so,' said the Hatter: 'as the things get used up.'

'But what happens when you come to the beginning again?' Alice ventured to ask.

'Suppose we change the subject,' the March Hare interrupted, yawning. 'I'm getting tired of this. I vote the young lady tells us a story.'

'I'm afraid I don't know one,' said Alice, rather alarmed at the proposal.

'Then the Dormouse shall!' they both cried. 'Wake up, Dormouse!' And they pinched it on both sides at once.

The Dormouse slowly opened his eyes. 'I wasn't asleep,' he said in a hoarse, feeble voice: 'I heard every word you fellows were saying.'

'Tell us a story!' said the March Hare.

'Yes, please do!' pleaded Alice.

'And be quick about it,' added the Hatter, 'or you'll be asleep again before it's done.'

'Once upon a time there were three little sisters,' the Dormouse began in a great hurry; 'and their names were Elsie, Lacie, and Tillie; and they lived at the bottom of a well —'

'What did they live on?' said Alice, who always took a great interest in questions of eating and drinking.

'They lived on treacle,' said the Dormouse, after thinking a minute or two.

'They couldn't have done that, you know,' Alice gently remarked; 'they'd have been ill.'

'So they were,' said the Dormouse; '*very* ill.'

Alice tried to fancy to herself what such an extraordinary way of living would be like, but it puzzled her too much, so she went on: 'But why did they live at the bottom of a well?'

'Take some more tea,' the March Hare said to Alice, very earnestly.

'I've had nothing yet,' Alice replied in an offended tone, 'so I can't take more.'

'You mean you can't take *less*,' said the Hatter: 'it's very easy to take *more* than nothing.'

'Nobody asked *your* opinion,' said Alice.

'Who's making personal remarks now?' the Hatter asked triumphantly.

Alice did not quite know what to say to this: so she helped herself to some tea and bread-and-butter, and then turned to the Dormouse, and repeated her question. 'Why did they live at the bottom of a well?'

The Dormouse again took a minute or two to think about it, and then said, 'It was a treacle-well.'

'There's no such thing!' Alice was beginning very angrily, but the Hatter and the March Hare went 'Sh! sh!' and the Dormouse sulkily remarked, 'If you can't be civil, you'd better finish the story for yourself.'

'No, please go on!' Alice said very humbly; 'I won't interrupt again. I dare say there may be *one*.'

'One, indeed!' said the Dormouse indignantly. However, he consented to go on. 'And so these three little sisters — they were learning to draw, you know —'

'What did they draw?' said Alice, quite forgetting her promise.

'Treacle,' said the Dormouse, without considering at all this time.

'I want a clean cup,' interrupted the Hatter: 'let's all move one place on.'

He moved on as he spoke, and the Dormouse followed him: the March Hare moved into the Dormouse's place, and Alice rather unwillingly took the place of the March Hare. The Hatter was the only one who got any advantage from the change: and Alice was a good deal worse off than before, as the March Hare had just upset the milk-jug into his plate.

Alice did not wish to offend the Dormouse again, so she began very cautiously: 'But I don't understand. Where did they draw the treacle from?'

'You can draw water out of a water-well,' said the Hatter; 'so I should think you could draw treacle out of a treacle-well — eh, stupid?'

'But they were *in* the well,' Alice said to the Dormouse, not choosing to notice this last remark.

'Of course they were,' said the Dormouse; '— well in.'

This answer so confused poor Alice, that she let the

Dormouse go on for some time without interrupting it.

'They were learning to draw,' the Dormouse went on, yawning and rubbing its eyes, for it was getting very sleepy; 'and they drew all manner of things — everything that begins with an M —'

'Why with an M?' said Alice.

'Why not?' said the March Hare.

Alice was silent.

The Dormouse had closed its eyes by this time, and was going off into a doze; but, on being pinched by the Hatter, it woke up again with a little shriek, and went on: '—that begins with an M, such as mouse-traps, and the moon, and memory, and muchness—you know you say things are "much of a muchness"—did you ever see such a thing as a drawing of a muchness?'

'Really, now you ask me,' said Alice, very much confused, 'I don't think—'

'Then you shouldn't talk,' said the Hatter.

This piece of rudeness was more than Alice could bear: she got up in great disgust, and walked off; the Dormouse fell asleep instantly, and neither of the others took the least notice of her going, though she looked back once or twice, half hoping that they would call after her: the last time she saw them, they were trying to put the Dormouse into the tea-pot.

'At any rate I'll never go *there* again!' said Alice as she picked her way through the wood. 'It's the stupidest tea-party I ever was at in all my life!'

Just as she said this, she noticed that one of the trees had a door leading right into it. 'That's very curious!' she thought. 'But everything's curious today. I think I may as well go in at once.' And in she went.

Once more she found herself in the long hall, and close to the little glass table. 'Now, I'll manage better this time,' she said to herself, and began by taking the little golden key, and unlocking the door that led into the garden. Then she set to work nibbling at the mushroom (she had kept a piece of it in her pocket) till she was about a foot high: then she walked down the little passage: and *then*—she found herself at last in the beautiful garden, among the bright flower-beds and the cool fountains.

CHAPTER VIII

The Queen's Croquet-Ground

A large rose-tree stood near the entrance of the garden: the roses growing on it were white, but there were three gardeners at it, busily painting them red. Alice thought this a very curious thing, and she went nearer
5 to watch them, and just as she came up to them she heard one of them say, 'Look out now, Five! Don't go splashing paint over me like that!'

'I couldn't help it,' said Five, in a sulky tone; 'Seven jogged my elbow.'

10 On which Seven looked up and said, 'That's right, Five! Always lay the blame on others!'

'*You'd* better not talk!' said Five. 'I heard the Queen say only yesterday you deserved to be beheaded!'

'What for?' said the one who had spoken first.

15 'That's none of *your* business, Two!' said Seven.

'Yes, it *is* his business!' said Five, 'and I'll tell him — it was for bringing the cook tulip-roots instead of onions.'

Seven flung down his brush, and had just begun 'Well, of all the unjust things —' when his eye chanced to fall
20 upon Alice, as she stood watching them, and he checked himself suddenly: the others looked round also, and all of them bowed low.

'Would you tell me,' said Alice, a little timidly 'why you are painting those roses?'

Five and Seven said nothing, but looked at Two. Two began in a low voice, 'Why the fact is, you see, Miss, this here ought to have been a *red* rose-tree, and we put a white one in by mistake; and if the Queen was to find it out, we should all have our heads cut off, you know. So you see, Miss, we're doing our best, afore she comes, to—' At this moment Five, who had been anxiously looking across the garden, called out 'The Queen! The Queen!' and the three gardeners instantly threw themselves flat upon their faces. There was a sound of many footsteps, and Alice looked round, eager to see the Queen.

First came ten soldiers carrying clubs; these were all shaped like the three gardeners, oblong and flat, with their hands and feet at the corners: next the ten courtiers; these were ornamented all over with diamonds, and walked two and two, as the soldiers did. After these came the royal children; there were ten of them, and the little dears came jumping merrily along hand in hand, in couples: they were all ornamented with hearts. Next came the guests, mostly Kings and Queens, and among them Alice recognised the White Rabbit: it was talking

in a hurried nervous manner, smiling at everything that was said, and went by without noticing her. Then followed the Knave of Hearts, carrying the King's crown on a crimson velvet cushion; and, last of all this grand
5 procession, came THE KING AND QUEEN OF HEARTS.

Alice was rather doubtful whether she ought not to lie down on her face like the three gardeners, but she could not remember ever having heard of such a rule at processions; 'and besides, what would be the use of a
10 procession,' thought she, 'if people had all to lie down upon their faces, so that they couldn't see it?' So she stood still where she was, and waited.

When the procession came opposite to Alice, they all stopped and looked at her, and the Queen said severely
15 'Who is this?' She said it to the Knave of Hearts, who only bowed and smiled in reply.

'Idiot!' said the Queen, tossing her head impatiently; and, turning to Alice, she went on, 'What's your name, child?'
20 'My name is Alice, so please your Majesty,' said Alice very politely; but she added, to herself, 'Why, they're only a pack of cards, after all. I needn't be afraid of them!'

'And who are *these*?' said the Queen, pointing to the
25 three gardeners who were lying round the rose-tree; for, you see, as they were lying on their faces, and the pattern on their backs was the same as the rest of the pack, she could not tell whether they were gardeners, or

soldiers, or courtiers, or three of her own children.

'How should *I* know?' said Alice, surprised at her own courage. 'It's no business of *mine*.'

The Queen turned crimson with fury, and, after glaring at her for a moment like a wild beast, screamed 'Off with her head! Off—'

'Nonsense!' said Alice, very loudly and decidedly, and the Queen was silent.

The King laid his hand upon her arm, and timidly said 'Consider, my dear: she is only a child!'

The Queen turned angrily away from him, and said to the Knave 'Turn them over!'

The Knave did so, very carefully, with one foot.

'Get up!' said the Queen, in a shrill, loud voice, and the three gardeners instantly jumped up, and began bowing to the King, the Queen, the royal children, and everybody else.

'Leave off that!' screamed the Queen. 'You make me giddy.' And then, turning to the rose-tree, she went on, 'What *have* you been doing here?'

'May it please your Majesty,' said Two, in a very humble tone, going down on one knee as he spoke, 'we were trying—'

'*I* see!' said the Queen, who had meanwhile been examining the roses. 'Off with their heads!' and the procession moved on, three of the soldiers remaining behind to execute the unfortunate gardeners, who ran to Alice for protection.

THE QUEEN'S CROQUET-GROUND

'You shan't be beheaded!' said Alice, and she put them into a large flower-pot that stood near. The three soldiers wandered about for a minute or two, looking for them, and then quietly marched off after the others.

5 'Are their heads off?' shouted the Queen.

'Their heads are gone, if it please your Majesty!' the soldiers shouted in reply.

'That's right!' shouted the Queen. 'Can you play croquet?'

10 The soldiers were silent, and looked at Alice, as the question was evidently meant for her.

'Yes!' shouted Alice.

'Come on, then!' roared the Queen, and Alice joined the procession, wondering very much what would happen next.

'It's — it's a very fine day!' said a timid voice at her side. She was walking by the White Rabbit, who was peeping anxiously into her face.

'Very,' said Alice: '— where's the Duchess?'

'Hush! Hush!' said the Rabbit in a low, hurried tone. He looked anxiously over his shoulder as he spoke, and then raised himself upon tiptoe, put his mouth close to her ear, and whispered 'She's under sentence of execution.'

'What for?' said Alice.

'Did you say "What a pity!"?' the Rabbit asked.

'No, I didn't,' said Alice: 'I don't think it's at all a pity. I said "What for?"'

'She boxed the Queen's ears —' the Rabbit began. Alice gave a little scream of laughter. 'Oh, hush!' the Rabbit whispered in a frightened tone. 'The Queen will hear you! You see, she came rather late, and the Queen said —'

'Get to your places!' shouted the Queen in a voice of thunder, and people began running about in all directions, tumbling up against each other; however, they got settled down in a minute or two, and the game began. Alice thought she had never seen such a curious croquet-ground in all her life; it was all ridges and furrows; the balls were live hedgehogs, the mallets live flamingoes, and the soldiers had to double themselves up and to stand on their hands and feet, to make the arches.

The chief difficulty Alice found at first was in managing her flamingo: she succeeded in getting its body tucked away, comfortably enough, under her arm, with its legs hanging down, but generally, just as she had got its neck nicely straightened out, and was going to give the hedgehog a blow with its head, it *would* twist itself round and look up in her face, with such a puzzled expression that she could not help bursting out laughing: and when she had got its head down, and was going to begin again, it was very provoking to find that the hedgehog had unrolled itself, and was in the act of crawling away: besides all this, there was generally a ridge or furrow in the way wherever she wanted to send the hedgehog to, and, as the doubled-up soldiers were always getting up and walking off to other parts of the ground, Alice soon came to the conclusion that it was a very difficult game indeed.

The players all played at once without waiting for turns, quarrelling all the while, and fighting for the hedgehogs; and in a very short time the Queen was in a furious passion, and went stamping about, and shouting

'Off with his head!' or 'Off with her head!' about once in a minute.

Alice began to feel very uneasy: to be sure, she had not as yet had any dispute with the Queen, but she knew that it might happen any minute, 'and then,' thought she, 'what would become of me? They're dreadfully fond of beheading people here; the great wonder is, that there's any one left alive!'

She was looking about for some way of escape, and wondering whether she could get away without being seen, when she noticed a curious appearance in the air: it puzzled her very much at first, but, after watching it a minute or two, she made it out to be a grin, and she said to herself 'It's the Cheshire Cat: now I shall have somebody to talk to.'

'How are you getting on?' said the Cat, as soon as there was mouth enough for it to speak with.

Alice waited till the eyes appeared, and then nodded. 'It's no use speaking to it,' she thought, 'till its ears have come, or at least one of them.' In another minute the whole head appeared, and then Alice put down her flamingo, and began an account of the game, feeling very glad she had someone to listen to her. The Cat seemed to think that there was enough of it now in sight, and no more of it appeared.

'I don't think they play at all fairly,' Alice began, in rather a complaining tone, 'and they all quarrel so dreadfully one can't hear oneself speak—and they don't seem to have any rules in particular; at least, if there are, nobody attends to them—and you've no idea how confusing it is all the things being alive; for instance, there's the arch I've got to go through next walking about at the other end of the ground—and I should have croqueted the Queen's hedgehog just now, only it ran away when it saw mine coming?'

'How do you like the Queen?' said the Cat in a low voice.

'Not at all,' said Alice: 'she's so extremely—' Just then she noticed that the Queen was close behind her, listening: so she went on, '—likely to win, that it's hardly worth while finishing the game.'

The Queen smiled and passed on.

'Who *are* you talking to?' said the King, coming up to Alice, and looking at the Cat's head with great curiosity.

'It's a friend of mine—a Cheshire Cat,' said Alice: 'allow me to introduce it.'

'I don't like the look of it at all,' said the King: 'however, it may kiss my hand if it likes.'

'I'd rather not,' the Cat remarked.

'Don't be impertinent,' said the King, 'and don't look at me like that!' He got behind Alice as he spoke.

'A cat may look at a king,' said Alice. 'I've read that in some book, but I don't remember where.'

'Well, it must be removed,' said the King very decidedly, and he called to the Queen, who was passing at the moment, 'My dear! I wish you would have this cat removed!'

The Queen had only one way of settling all difficulties, great or small. 'Off with his head!' she said, without even looking round.

'I'll fetch the executioner myself,' said the King eagerly, and he hurried off.

Alice thought she might as well go back, and see how the game was going on, as she heard the Queen's voice in the distance, screaming with passion. She had already heard her sentence three of the players to be executed for having missed their turns, and she did not like the look of things at all, as the game was in such confusion that she never knew whether it was her turn or not. So she went in search of her hedgehog.

The hedgehog was engaged in a fight with another hedgehog, which seemed to Alice an excellent opportunity for croqueting one of them with the other: the only difficulty was, that her flamingo was gone across to the other side of the garden, where Alice could see it trying in a helpless sort of way to fly up into a tree.

By the time she had caught the flamingo and brought it back, the fight was over, and both the hedgehogs were out of sight: 'but it doesn't matter much,' thought Alice, 'as all the arches are gone from this side of the ground.' So she tucked it away under her arm, that it might not escape again, and went back for a little more conversation with her friend.

When she got back to the Cheshire Cat, she was sur-

THE QUEEN'S CROQUET-GROUND

prised to find quite a large crowd collected round it: there was a dispute going on between the executioner, the King, and the Queen, who were all talking at once, while all the rest were quite silent, and looked very uncomfortable.

The moment Alice appeared, she was appealed to by all three to settle the question, and they repeated their arguments to her, though, as they all spoke at once, she found it very hard indeed to make out exactly what they said.

The executioner's argument was, that you couldn't cut off a head unless there was a body to cut it off from: that he had never had to do such a thing before, and he wasn't going to begin at *his* time of life.

The King's argument was, that anything that had a head could be beheaded, and that you weren't to talk nonsense.

The Queen's argument was, that if something wasn't done about it in less than no time she'd have everybody executed, all round. (It was this last remark that had made the whole party look so grave and anxious.)

Alice could think of nothing else to say but 'It belongs to the Duchess: you'd better ask *her* about it.'

'She's in prison,' the Queen said to the executioner: 'fetch her here.' And the executioner went off like an arrow.

The Cat's head began fading away the moment he was gone, and, by the time he had come back with the Duchess, it had entirely disappeared; so the King and the executioner ran wildly up and down looking for it, while the rest of the party went back to the game.

CHAPTER IX

The Mock Turtle's Story

'You can't think how glad I am to see you again, you dear old thing!' said the Duchess, as she tucked her arm affectionately into Alice's, and they walked off together.

Alice was very glad to find her in such a pleasant temper, and thought to herself that perhaps it was only the pepper that had made her so savage when they met in the kitchen.

'When *I'm* a Duchess,' she said to herself, (not in a very hopeful tone though), 'I won't have any pepper in my kitchen *at all*. Soup does very well without—Maybe it's always pepper that makes people hot-tempered,' she went on, very much pleased at having found out a new kind of rule, 'and vinegar that makes them sour—and camomile that makes them bitter—and—and barley-sugar and such things that make children sweet-tempered. I only wish people knew *that*: then they wouldn't be so stingy about it, you know—'

She had quite forgotten the Duchess by this time, and was a little startled when she heard her voice close to her ear. 'You're thinking about something, my dear, and that makes you forget to talk. I can't tell you just now what the moral of that is, but I shall remember it in a bit.'

'Perhaps it hasn't one,' Alice ventured to remark.

'Tut, tut, child!' said the Duchess. 'Everything's got a moral, if only you can find it.' And she squeezed herself up closer to Alice's side as she spoke.

Alice did not much like keeping so close to her: first, because the Duchess was *very* ugly; and secondly, because she was exactly the right height to rest her chin upon Alice's shoulder, and it was an uncomfortably sharp chin. However, she did not like to be rude, so she bore it as well as she could.

'The game's going on rather better now,' she said, by way of keeping up the conversation a little.

'' Tis so,' said the Duchess: 'and the moral of that is—"Oh, 'tis love, 'tis love, that makes the world go round!"'

'Somebody said,' Alice whispered, 'that it's done by everybody minding their own business!'

'Ah, well! It means much the same thing,' said the Duchess, digging her sharp little chin into Alice's shoulder as she added, 'and the moral of *that* is—"Take care of the sense, and the sounds will take care of themselves."'

'How fond she is of finding morals in things!' Alice thought to herself.

THE MOCK TURTLE'S STORY

'I dare say you're wondering why I don't put my arm round your waist,' the Duchess said after a pause: 'the reason is, that I'm doubtful about the temper of your flamingo. Shall I try the experiment?'

5 'He might bite,' Alice cautiously replied, not feeling at all anxious to have the experiment tried.

'Very true,' said the Duchess: 'flamingoes and mustard both bite. And the moral of that is—"Birds of a feather flock together."'

10 'Only mustard isn't a bird,' Alice remarked.

'Right, as usual,' said the Duchess: 'what a clear way you have of putting things!'

'It's a mineral, I *think*,' said Alice.

'Of course it is,' said the Duchess, who seemed ready 15 to agree to everything that Alice said; 'there's a large mustard-mine near here. And the moral of that is— "The more there is of mine, the less there is of yours."'

'Oh, I know!' exclaimed Alice, who had not attended to this last remark, 'it's a vegetable. It doesn't look like 20 one, but it is.'

'I quite agree with you,' said the Duchess; 'and the moral of that is—"Be what you would seem to be"—or if you'd like it put more simply—"Never imagine yourself not to be otherwise than what it might appear to others 25 that what you were or might have been was not otherwise than what you had been would have appeared to them to be otherwise."'

'I think I should understand that better,' Alice said

very politely, 'if I had it written down: but I can't quite follow it as you say it.'

'That's nothing to what I could say if I chose,' the Duchess replied, in a pleased tone.

'Pray don't trouble yourself to say it any longer than that,' said Alice.

'Oh, don't talk about trouble!' said the Duchess. 'I make you a present of everything I've said as yet.'

'A cheap sort of present!' thought Alice. 'I'm glad they don't give birthday presents like that!' But she did not venture to say it out loud.

'Thinking again?' the Duchess asked, with another dig of her sharp little chin.

'I've a right to think,' said Alice sharply, for she was beginning to feel a little worried.

'Just about as much right,' said the Duchess, 'as pigs have to fly; and the m —'

But here, to Alice's great surprise, the Duchess's voice died away, even in the middle of her favourite word 'moral,' and the arm that was linked into hers began to tremble. Alice looked up, and there stood the Queen in front of them, with her arms folded, frowning like a thunderstorm.

'A fine day, your Majesty!' the Duchess began in a low, weak voice.

'Now, I give you fair warning,' shouted the Queen, stamping on the ground as she spoke; 'either you or your head must be off, and that in about half no time!

THE MOCK TURTLE'S STORY

Take your choice!'

The Duchess took her choice, and was gone in a moment.

'Let's go on with the game,' the Queen said to Alice; and Alice was too much frightened to say a word, but slowly followed her back to the croquet-ground.

The other guests had taken advantage of the Queen's absence, and were resting in the shade: however, the moment they saw her, they hurried back to the game, the Queen merely remarking that a moment's delay would cost them their lives.

All the time they were playing the Queen never left off quarrelling with the other players, and shouting 'Off with his head!' or 'Off with her head!' Those whom she sentenced were taken into custody by the soldiers, who of course had to leave off being arches to do this, so that by the end of half an hour or so there were no arches left, and all the players, except the King, the Queen, and Alice, were in custody and under sentence of execution.

Then the Queen left off, quite out of breath, and said to Alice, 'Have you seen the Mock Turtle yet?'

'No,' said Alice. 'I don't even know what a Mock Turtle is.'

'It's the thing Mock Turtle Soup is made from,' said the Queen.

'I never saw one, or heard of one,' said Alice.

'Come on, then,' said the Queen, 'and he shall tell you

his history.'

As they walked off together, Alice heard the King say in a low voice, to the company generally, 'You are all pardoned.' 'Come, *that's* a good thing!' she said to herself, for she had felt quite unhappy at the number of executions the Queen had ordered.

They very soon came upon a Gryphon, lying fast asleep in the sun. (If you don't know what a Gryphon is, look at the picture.) 'Up, lazy thing!' said the Queen, 'and take this young lady to see the Mock Turtle, and to hear his history. I must go back and see after some executions I have ordered'; and she walked off, leaving Alice alone with the Gryphon. Alice did not quite like the look of the creature, but on the whole she thought it would be quite as safe to stay with it as to go after that savage Queen: so she waited.

The Gryphon sat up and rubbed its eyes: then it watched the Queen till she was out of sight: then it chuckled. 'What fun!' said the Gryphon, half to itself, half to Alice.

'What *is* the fun?' said Alice.

'Why, *she*,' said the Gryphon. 'It's all her fancy, that: they never executes nobody, you know. Come on!'

'Everybody says "come on!" here,' thought Alice, as she went slowly after it: 'I never was so ordered about in all my life, never!'

They had not gone far before they saw the Mock Turtle in the distance, sitting sad and lonely on a little ledge of rock, and, as they came nearer, Alice could hear him sighing as if his heart would break. She pitied him deeply. 'What is his sorrow?' she asked the Gryphon, and the Gryphon answered, very nearly in the same words as before, 'It's all his fancy, that: he hasn't got no sorrow, you know. Come on!'

So they went up to the Mock Turtle, who looked at them with large eyes full of tears, but said nothing.

'This here young lady,' said the Gryphon, 'she wants for to know your history, she do.'

'I'll tell it her,' said the Mock Turtle in a deep, hollow tone: 'sit down, both of you, and don't speak a word till I've finished.'

So they sat down, and nobody spoke for some minutes. Alice thought to herself, 'I don't see how he can *ever* finish, if he doesn't begin.' But she waited patiently.

'Once,' said the Mock Turtle at last, with a deep sigh, 'I was a real Turtle.'

These words were followed by a very long silence, broken only by an occasional exclamation of 'Hjckrrh!' from the Gryphon, and the constant heavy sobbing of the Mock Turtle. Alice was very nearly getting up and saying, 'Thank you, sir, for your interesting story,' but she could not help thinking there *must* be more to come, so she sat still and said nothing.

'When we were little,' the Mock Turtle went on at last, more calmly, though still sobbing a little now and then, 'we went to school in the sea. The master was an old Turtle — we used to call him Tortoise — '

THE MOCK TURTLE'S STORY

'Why did you call him Tortoise, if he wasn't one?' Alice asked.

'We called him Tortoise because he taught us,' said the Mock Turtle angrily: 'really you are very dull!'

'You ought to be ashamed of yourself for asking such a simple question,' added the Gryphon; and then they both sat silent and looked at poor Alice, who felt ready to sink into the earth. At last the Gryphon said to the Mock Turtle, 'Drive on, old fellow! Don't be all day about it!' and he went on in these words:

'Yes, we went to school in the sea, though you mayn't believe it—'

'I never said I didn't!' interrupted Alice.

'You did,' said the Mock Turtle.

'Hold your tongue!' added the Gryphon, before Alice could speak again. The Mock Turtle went on.

'We had the best of educations—in fact, we went to school every day—'

'*I've* been to a day-school, too,' said Alice; 'you needn't be so proud as all that.'

'With extras?' asked the Mock Turtle a little anxiously.

'Yes,' said Alice, 'we learned French and music.'

'And washing?' said the Mock Turtle.

'Certainly not!' said Alice indignantly.

'Ah! then yours wasn't a really good school,' said the Mock Turtle in a tone of great relief. 'Now at *ours* they had at the end of the bill, "French, music, *and washing* — extra."'

'You couldn't have wanted it much,' said Alice; 'living at the bottom of the sea.'

'I couldn't afford to learn it,' said the Mock Turtle with a sigh. 'I only took the regular course.'

'What was that?' inquired Alice.

'Reeling and Writhing, of course, to begin with,' the Mock Turtle replied; 'and then the different branches of Arithmetic — Ambition, Distraction, Uglification, and Derision.'

'I never heard of "Uglification,"' Alice ventured to say. 'What is it?'

The Gryphon lifted up both its paws in surprise. 'What! Never heard of uglifying!' it exclaimed. 'You know what to beautify is, I suppose?'

'Yes,' said Alice doubtfully: 'it means — to — make — anything — prettier.'

'Well, then,' the Gryphon went on, 'if you don't know what to uglify is, you *are* a simpleton.'

Alice did not feel encouraged to ask any more questions about it, so she turned to the Mock Turtle, and said 'What else had you to learn?'

'Well, there was Mystery,' the Mock Turtle replied, counting off the subjects on his flappers, '— Mystery, ancient and modern, with Seaography: then Drawling — the Drawling-master was an old conger-eel, that used to come once a week: *he* taught us Drawling, Stretching, and Fainting in Coils.'

'What was *that* like?' said Alice.

'Well, I can't show it you myself,' the Mock Turtle said: 'I'm too stiff. And the Gryphon never learnt it.'

'Hadn't time,' said the Gryphon: 'I went to the Classical master, though. He was an old crab, *he* was.'

'I never went to him,' the Mock Turtle said with a sigh: 'he taught Laughing and Grief, they used to say.'

'So he did, so he did,' said the Gryphon, sighing in his turn; and both creatures hid their faces in their paws.

'And how many hours a day did you do lessons?' said Alice, in a hurry to change the subject.

'Ten hours the first day,' said the Mock Turtle: 'nine the next, and so on.'

'What a curious plan!' exclaimed Alice.

'That's the reason they're called lessons,' the Gryphon remarked: 'because they lessen from day to day.'

This was quite a new idea to Alice, and she thought it over a little before she made her next remark. 'Then the eleventh day must have been a holiday?'

'Of course it was,' said the Mock Turtle.

'And how did you manage on the twelfth?' Alice went on eagerly.

'That's enough about lessons,' the Gryphon interrupted in a very decided tone: 'tell her something about the games now.'

CHAPTER X

The Lobster Quadrille

The Mock Turtle sighed deeply, and drew the back of one flapper across his eyes. He looked at Alice, and tried to speak, but for a minute or two sobs choked his voice. 'Same as if he had a bone in his throat,' said the Gryphon: and it set to work shaking him and punching him in the back. At last the Mock Turtle recovered his voice, and, with tears running down his cheeks, he went on again: —

'You may not have lived much under the sea —' ('I haven't,' said Alice) — 'and perhaps you were never even introduced to a lobster —' (Alice began to say 'I once tasted —' but checked herself hastily, and said 'No, never') '— so you can have no idea what a delightful thing a Lobster Quadrille is!'

'No, indeed,' said Alice. 'What sort of a dance is it?'

'Why,' said the Gryphon, 'you first form into a line along the sea-shore —'

'Two lines!' cried the Mock Turtle. 'Seals, turtles, salmon, and so on; then, when you've cleared all the jelly-fish out of the way —'

'*That* generally takes some time,' interrupted the Gryphon.

'— you advance twice —'

'Each with a lobster as a partner!' cried the Gryphon.

'Of course,' the Mock Turtle said: 'advance twice, set to partners —'

'— change lobsters, and retire in same order,' continued the Gryphon.

'Then, you know,' the Mock Turtle went on, 'you throw the —'

'The lobsters!' shouted the Gryphon, with a bound into the air.

'— as far out to sea as you can —'

'Swim after them!' screamed the Gryphon.

'Turn a somersault in the sea!' cried the Mock Turtle, capering wildly about.

'Change lobsters again!' yelled the Gryphon.

'Back to land again, and that's all the first figure,' said the Mock Turtle, suddenly dropping his voice; and the two creatures, who had been jumping about like mad things all this time, sat down again very sadly and quietly, and looked at Alice.

'It must be a very pretty dance,' said Alice timidly.

'Would you like to see a little of it?' said the Mock Turtle.

'Very much indeed,'

said Alice.

'Come, let's try the first figure!' said the Mock Turtle to the Gryphon. 'We can do without lobsters, you know. Which shall sing?'

'Oh, *you* sing,' said the Gryphon. 'I've forgotten the words.'

So they began solemnly dancing round and round Alice, every now and then treading on her toes when they passed too close, and waving their forepaws to mark the time, while the Mock Turtle sang this, very slowly and sadly: —

"'*Will you walk a little faster?*" *said a whiting to a snail.*
"*There's a porpoise close behind us, and he's treading on
   my tail.*
See how eagerly the lobsters and the turtles all advance!
*They are waiting on the shingle — will you come and join
   the dance?*
   *Will you, won't you, will you, won't you, will you join
     the dance?*
   *Will you, won't you, will you, won't you, won't you join
     the dance?*

'"*You can really have no notion how delightful it will be
*When they take us up and throw us, with the lobsters, out
   to sea!*"
But the snail replied "*Too far, too far!*" *and gave a look
   askance —*
*Said he thanked the whiting kindly, but he would not join
   the dance.*
   *Would not, could not, would not, could not, would not join
     the dance.*

THE LOBSTER QUADRILLE

Would not, could not, would not, could not, could not join the dance.

' "What matters it how far we go?" his scaly friend replied.
"There is another shore, you know, upon the other side.
5 *The further off from England the nearer is to France —
Then turn not pale, beloved snail, but come and join the dance.
Will you, won't you, will you, won't you, will you join the dance?*
10 *Will you, won't you, will you, won't you, won't you join the dance?"*'

'Thank you, it's a very interesting dance to watch,' said Alice, feeling very glad that it was over at last: 'and I do so like that curious song about the whiting!'
15 'Oh, as to the whiting,' said the Mock Turtle, 'they — you've seen them, of course?'

'Yes,' said Alice, 'I've often seen them at dinn—' she checked herself hastily.

'I don't know where Dinn may be,' said the Mock
20 Turtle, 'but if you've seen them so often, of course you know what they're like.'

'I believe so,' Alice replied thoughtfully. 'They have their tails in their mouths — and they're all over crumbs.'

'You're wrong about the crumbs,' said the Mock
25 Turtle: 'crumbs would all wash off in the sea. But they *have* their tails in their mouths; and the reason is —' here the Mock Turtle yawned and shut his eyes. — 'Tell her about the reason and all that,' he said to the Gryphon.

'The reason is,' said the Gryphon, 'that they *would* go with the lobsters to the dance. So they got thrown out to sea. So they had to fall a long way. So they got their tails fast in their mouths. So they couldn't get them out again. That's all.'

'Thank you,' said Alice, 'it's very interesting. I never knew so much about a whiting before.'

'I can tell you more than that, if you like,' said the Gryphon. 'Do you know why it's called a whiting?'

'I never thought about it,' said Alice. 'Why?'

'*It does the boots and shoes*,' the Gryphon replied very solemnly.

Alice was thoroughly puzzled. 'Does the boots and shoes!' she repeated in a wondering tone.

'Why, what are *your* shoes done with?' said the Gryphon. 'I mean, what makes them so shiny?'

Alice looked down at them, and considered a little before she gave her answer. 'They're done with blacking, I believe.'

'Boots and shoes under the sea,' the Gryphon went on in a deep voice, 'are done with whiting. Now you know.'

'And what are they made of?' Alice asked in a tone of great curiosity.

'Soles and eels, of course,' the Gryphon replied rather impatiently: 'any shrimp could have told you that.'

'If I'd been the whiting,' said Alice, whose thoughts were still running on the song, 'I'd have said to the

THE LOBSTER QUADRILLE

porpoise, "Keep back, please: we don't want *you* with us!"'

'They were obliged to have him with them,' the Mock Turtle said: 'no wise fish would go anywhere without a porpoise.'

'Wouldn't it really?' said Alice in a tone of great surprise.

'Of course not,' said the Mock Turtle: 'why, if a fish came to *me*, and told me he was going a journey, I should say "With what porpoise?"'

'Don't you mean "purpose"?' said Alice.

'I mean what I say,' the Mock Turtle replied in an offended tone. And the Gryphon added 'Come, let's hear some of *your* adventures.'

'I could tell you my adventures — beginning from this morning,' said Alice a little timidly: 'but it's no use going back to yesterday, because I was a different person then.'

'Explain all that,' said the Mock Turtle.

'No, no! The adventures first,' said the Gryphon in an impatient tone: 'explanations take such a dreadful time.'

So Alice began telling them her adventures from the time when she first saw the White Rabbit. She was a little nervous about it just at first, the two creatures got so close to her, one on each side, and opened their eyes and mouths so *very* wide, but she gained courage as she went on. Her listeners were perfectly quiet till she got to the part about her repeating '*You are old, Father William*,' to the Caterpillar, and the words all coming different, and then the Mock Turtle drew a long breath, and said 'That's very curious.'

'It's all about as curious as it can be,' said the Gryphon.

'It all came different!' the Mock Turtle repeated thoughtfully. 'I should like to hear her try and repeat something now. Tell her to begin.' He looked at the Gryphon as if he thought it had some kind of authority over Alice.

'Stand up and repeat "*'Tis the voice of the sluggard,*"' said the Gryphon.

'How the creatures order one about, and make one repeat lessons!' thought Alice; 'I might as well be at school at once.' However, she got up, and began to repeat it, but her head was so full of the Lobster Quadrille, that she hardly knew what she was saying, and the words came very queer indeed: —

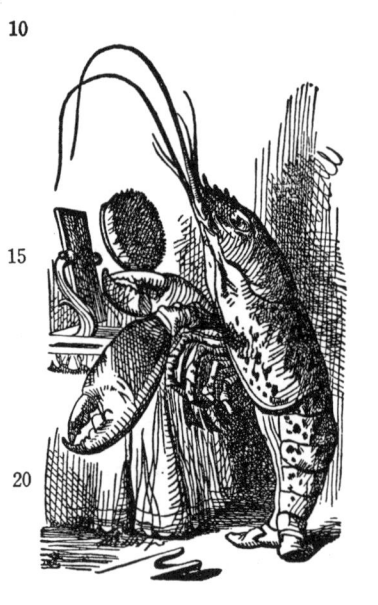

''Tis the voice of the Lobster; I heard him declare,
"You have baked me too brown, I must sugar my hair."
As a duck with its eyelids, so he with his nose
Trims his belt and his buttons, and turns out his toes.'

> *When the sands are all dry, he is gay as a lark,*
> *And will talk in contemptuous tones of the Shark.*
> *But, when the tide rises and sharks are around,*
> *His voice has a timid and tremulous sound.*

'That's different from what *I* used to say when I was a child,' said the Gryphon.

'Well, I never heard it before,' said the Mock Turtle; 'but it sounds uncommon nonsense.'

Alice said nothing; she had sat down with her face in her hands, wondering if anything would *ever* happen in a natural way again.

'I should like to have it explained,' said the Mock Turtle.

'She can't explain it,' said the Gryphon hastily. 'Go on with the next verse.'

'But about his toes?' the Mock Turtle persisted. 'How *could* he turn them out with his nose, you know?'

'It's the first position in dancing,' Alice said; but was dreadfully puzzled by the whole thing, and longed to change the subject.

'Go on with the next verse,' the Gryphon repeated impatiently: 'it begins "*I passed by his garden.*"'

Alice did not dare to disobey, though she felt sure it would all come wrong, and she went on in a trembling voice:—

> '*I passed by his garden, and marked, with one eye,*
> *How the Owl and the Panther were sharing a pie—*'
> *The Panther took pie-crust, and gravy, and meat,*
> *While the Owl had the dish as its share of the treat.*

When the pie was all finished, the Owl, as a boon,
Was kindly permitted to pocket the spoon:
While the Panther received knife and fork with a growl,
And concluded the banquet— 5

'What *is* the use of repeating all that stuff,' the Mock Turtle interrupted, 'if you don't explain it as you go on? It's by far the most confusing thing *I* ever heard!'

'Yes, I think you'd better leave off,' said the Gryphon: and Alice was only too glad to do so. 10

'Shall we try another figure of the Lobster Quadrille?' the Gryphon went on. 'Or would you like the Mock Turtle to sing you a song?'

'Oh, a song, please, if the Mock Turtle would be so kind,' Alice replied, so eagerly that the Gryphon said, in 15 a rather offended tone, 'Hm! No accounting for tastes! Sing her "*Turtle Soup*," will you, old fellow?'

The Mock Turtle sighed deeply, and began, in a voice sometimes choked with sobs, to sing this:—

'Beautiful Soup, so rich and green, 20
Waiting in a hot tureen!
Who for such dainties would not stoop?
Soup of the evening, beautiful Soup!
Soup of the evening, beautiful Soup!
  Beau—ootiful Soo—oop! 25
  Beau—ootiful Soo—oop!
Soo—oop of the e—e—evening,
  Beautiful, beautiful Soup!

THE LOBSTER QUADRILLE

> *'Beautiful Soup! Who cares for fish,*
> *Game, or any other dish?*
> *Who would not give all else for two p*
> *ennyworth only of beautiful Soup?*
> *Pennyworth only of beautiful Soup?*
> *Beau — ootiful Soo — oop!*
> *Beau — ootiful Soo — oop!*
> *Soo — oop of the e — e — evening,*
> *Beautiful, beauti — FUL SOUP!'*

'Chorus again!' cried the Gryphon, and the Mock Turtle had just begun to repeat it, when a cry of 'The trial's beginning!' was heard in the distance.

'Come on!' cried the Gryphon, and, taking Alice by the hand, it hurried off, without waiting for the end of the song.

'What trial is it?' Alice panted as she ran; but the Gryphon only answered 'Come on!' and ran the faster, while more and more faintly came, carried on the breeze that followed them, the melancholy words: —

> *'Soo — oop of the e — e — evening,*
> *Beautiful, beautiful Soup!'*

CHAPTER XI

Who Stole the Tarts?

The King and Queen of Hearts were seated on their throne when they arrived, with a great crowd assembled about them—all sorts of little birds and beasts, as well as the whole pack of cards: the Knave was standing before them, in chains, with a soldier on each side to guard him; and near the King was the White Rabbit, with a trumpet in one hand, and a scroll of parchment in the other. In the very middle of the court was a table, with a large dish of tarts upon it: they looked so good, that it made Alice quite hungry to look at them—'I wish they'd get the trial done,' she thought, 'and hand round the refreshments!' But there seemed to be no chance of this, so she began looking at everything about her, to pass away the time.

Alice had never been in a court of justice before, but she had read about them in books, and she was quite pleased to find that she knew the name of nearly everything there. 'That's the judge,' she said to herself, 'because of his great wig.'

The judge, by the way, was the King; and as he wore his crown over the wig, (look at the frontispiece if you want to see how he did it,) he did not look at all comfortable, and it was certainly not becoming.

'And that's the jury-box,' thought Alice, 'and those

twelve creatures,' (she was obliged to say 'creatures,' you see, because some of them were animals, and some were birds,) 'I suppose they are the jurors.' She said this last word two or three times over to herself, being rather proud of it: for she thought, and rightly too, that very few little girls of her age knew the meaning of it at all. However, 'jury-men' would have done just as well.

The twelve jurors were all writing very busily on slates. 'What are they doing?' Alice whispered to the Gryphon. 'They can't have anything to put down yet, before the trial's begun.'

'They're putting down their names,' the Gryphon whispered in reply, 'for fear they should forget them before the end of the trial.'

'Stupid things!' Alice began in a loud, indignant voice, but she stopped hastily, for the White Rabbit cried out, 'Silence in the court!' and the King put on his spectacles and looked anxiously round, to make out who was talking.

Alice **could** see, as well as if she were looking over their shoulders, that all the jurors were writing down 'stupid things!' on their slates, and she could even make out that one of them didn't know how to spell 'stupid,' and that he had to ask his neighbour to tell him. 'A nice muddle their slates'll be in before the trial's over!' thought Alice.

One of the jurors had a pencil that squeaked. This, of course, Alice could *not* stand, and she went round the court and got behind him, and very soon found an opportunity of taking it away. She did it so quickly that the poor little juror (it was Bill, the Lizard) could not make out at all what had become of it; so, after hunting all about for it, he was obliged to write with one finger for the rest of the day; and this was of very little use, as it left no mark on the slate.

'Herald, read the accusation!' said the King.

On this the White Rabbit blew three blasts on the trumpet, and then unrolled the parchment scroll, and read as follows:—

> '*The Queen of Hearts, she made some tarts,*
>   *All on a summer day:*
> *The Knave of Hearts, he stole those tarts,*
>   *And took them quite away!*'

'Consider your verdict,' the King said to the jury.

'Not yet, not yet!' the Rabbit hastily interrupted. 'There's a great deal to come before that!'

'Call the first witness,' said the King; and the White Rabbit blew three blasts on the trumpet, and called out, 'First witness!'

The first witness was the Hatter. He came in with a

teacup in one hand and a piece of bread-and-butter in the other. 'I beg pardon, your Majesty,' he began, 'for bringing these in: but I hadn't quite finished my tea when I was sent for.'

'You ought to have finished,' said the King. 'When did you begin?'

The Hatter looked at the March Hare, who had followed him into the court, arm-in-arm with the Dormouse. 'Fourteenth of March, I *think* it was,' he said.

'Fifteenth,' said the March Hare.

'Sixteenth,' added the Dormouse.

'Write that down,' the King said to the jury, and the jury eagerly wrote down all three dates on their slates, and then added them up, and reduced the answer to shillings and pence.

'Take off your hat,' the King said to the Hatter.

'It isn't mine,' said the Hatter.

'*Stolen!*' the King exclaimed, turning to the jury, who instantly made a memorandum of the fact.

'I keep them to sell,' the Hatter added as an explanation: 'I've none of my own. I'm a hatter.'

Here the Queen put on her spectacles, and began staring at the Hatter, who turned pale and fidgeted.

'Give your evidence,' said the King; 'and don't be nervous, or I'll have you executed on the spot.'

This did not seem to encourage the witness at all: he kept shifting from one foot to the other, looking uneasily at the Queen, and in his confusion he bit a large piece out of his teacup instead of the bread-and-butter.

Just at this moment Alice felt a very curious sensation, which puzzled her a good deal until she made out what it was: she was beginning to grow larger again, and she thought at first she would get up and leave the court; but on second thoughts she decided to remain where she was as long as there was room for her.

'I wish you wouldn't squeeze so,' said the Dormouse, who was sitting next to her. 'I can hardly breathe.'

'I can't help it,' said Alice very meekly: 'I'm growing.'

'You've no right to grow *here*,' said the Dormouse.

'Don't talk nonsense,' said Alice more boldly: 'you know you're growing too.'

'Yes, but *I* grow at a reasonable pace,' said the Dormouse: 'not in that ridiculous fashion.' And he got up very sulkily and crossed over to the other side of the court.

All this time the Queen had never left off staring at the Hatter, and, just as the Dormouse crossed the court, she said to one of the officers of the court, 'Bring me the list of the singers in the last concert!' on which the wretched Hatter trembled so, that he shook both his shoes off.

'Give your evidence,' the King repeated angrily, 'or I'll

have you executed, whether you're nervous or not.'

'I'm a poor man, your Majesty,' the Hatter began, in a trembling voice, '— and I hadn't begun my tea — not above a week or so — and what with the bread-and-butter getting so thin — and the twinkling of the tea —'

'The twinkling of the *what*?' said the King.

'It *began* with the tea,' the Hatter replied.

'Of course twinkling begins with a T!' said the King sharply. 'Do you take me for a dunce? Go on!'

'I'm a poor man,' the Hatter went on, 'and most things twinkled after that — only the March Hare said —'

'I didn't!' the March Hare interrupted in a great hurry.

'You did!' said the Hatter.

'I deny it!' said the March Hare.

'He denies it,' said the King: 'leave out that part.'

'Well, at any rate, the Dormouse said —' the Hatter went on, looking anxiously round to see if he would deny it too: but the Dormouse denied nothing, being fast asleep.

'After that,' continued the Hatter, 'I cut some more bread-and-butter —'

'But what did the Dormouse say?' one of the jury asked.

'That I can't remember,' said the Hatter.

'You *must* remember,' remarked the King, 'or I'll have you executed.'

The miserable Hatter dropped his teacup and bread-and-butter, and went down on one knee. 'I'm a poor man, your Majesty,' he began.

'You're a *very* poor *speaker*,' said the King.

Here one of the guinea-pigs cheered, and was immediately suppressed by the officers of the court. (As that is rather a hard word, I will just explain to you how it was done. They had a large canvas bag, which tied up at the mouth with strings: into this they slipped the guinea-pig, head first, and then sat upon it.)

'I'm glad I've seen that done,' thought Alice. 'I've so often read in the newspapers, at the end of trials, "There was some attempt at applause, which was immediately suppressed by the officers of the court," and I never understood what it meant till now.'

'If that's all you know about it, you may stand down,' continued the King.

'I can't go no lower,' said the Hatter: 'I'm on the floor, as it is.'

'Then you may *sit* down,' the King replied.

Here the other guinea-pig cheered, and was suppressed.

'Come, that finishes the guinea-pigs!' thought Alice. 'Now we shall get on better.'

'I'd rather finish my tea,' said the Hatter, with an anxious look at the Queen, who was reading the list of singers.

'You may go,' said the King, and the Hatter hurriedly left the court, without even waiting to put his shoes on.

'—and just take his head off outside,' the Queen added to one of the officers: but the Hatter was out of sight before the officer could get to the door.

'Call the next witness!' said the King.

5 The next witness was the Duchess's cook. She carried the pepper-box in her hand, and Alice guessed who it was, even before she got into the court, 10 by the way the people near the door began sneezing all at once.

'Give your evidence,' said the King.

'Shan't,' said the cook.

The King looked anxiously at the White Rabbit, who 15 said in a low voice, 'Your Majesty must cross-examine *this* witness.'

'Well, if I must, I must,' the King said, with a melancholy air, and, after folding his arms and frowning at the cook till his eyes were nearly out of sight, he said in a 20 deep voice, 'What are tarts made of?'

'Pepper, mostly,' said the cook.

'Treacle,' said a sleepy voice behind her.

'Collar that Dormouse,' the Queen shrieked out. 'Behead that Dormouse! Turn that Dormouse out of court! 25 Suppress him! Pinch him! Off with his whiskers!'

For some minutes the whole court was in confusion, getting the Dormouse turned out, and, by the time they had settled down again, the cook had disappeared.

'Never mind!' said the King, with an air of great relief. 'Call the next witness.' And he added in an undertone to the Queen, 'Really, my dear, *you* must cross-examine the next witness. It quite makes my forehead ache!'

Alice watched the White Rabbit as he fumbled over the list, feeling very curious to see what the next witness would be like, ' — for they haven't got much evidence *yet*,' she said to herself. Imagine her surprise, when the White Rabbit read out, at the top of his shrill little voice, the name ' Alice!'

CHAPTER XII

Alice's Evidence

'Here!' cried Alice, quite forgetting in the flurry of the moment how large she had grown in the last few minutes, and she jumped up in such a hurry that she tipped over the jury-box with the edge of her skirt, upsetting all the jurymen on to the heads of the crowd below, and there they lay sprawling about, reminding her very much of a globe of goldfish she had accidentally upset the week before.

'Oh, I *beg* your pardon!' she exclaimed in a tone of great dismay, and began picking them up again as quickly as she could, for the accident of the goldfish kept running in her head, and she had a vague sort of idea that they must be collected at once and put back into the jury-box, or they would die.

'The trial cannot proceed,' said the King in a very grave voice, 'until all the jurymen are back in their proper places — *all*,' he repeated with great emphasis, looking hard at Alice as he said so.

Alice looked at the jury-box, and saw that, in her haste, she had put the Lizard in head downwards, and the poor little thing was waving its tail about in a melancholy way, being quite unable to move. She soon got it out again, and put it right; 'not that it signifies much,' she said to herself; 'I should think it would be *quite* as much use in the trial one way up as the other.'

As soon as the jury had a little recovered from the shock of being upset, and their slates and pencils had been found and handed back to them, they set to work very diligently to write out a history of the accident, all except the Lizard, who seemed too much overcome to do anything but sit with its mouth open, gazing up into the roof of the court.

'What do you know about this business?' the King said to Alice.

'Nothing,' said Alice.

'Nothing *whatever*?' persisted the King.

'Nothing whatever,' said Alice.

'That's very important,' the King said, turning to the jury. They were just beginning to write this down on their slates, when the White Rabbit interrupted: '*Un*important, your Majesty means, of course,' he said in a very respectful tone, but frowning and making faces at him as he spoke.

'*Un*important, of course, I meant,' the King hastily said, and went on to himself in an undertone, 'important — unimportant — unimportant — important — ' as if he were trying which word sounded best.

Some of the jury wrote it down 'important,' and some 'unimportant.' Alice could see this, as she was near enough to look over their slates; 'but it doesn't matter a bit,' she thought to herself.

At this moment the King, who had been for some time busily writing in his note-book, called out 'Silence!' and read out from his book, 'Rule Forty-two. *All persons more than a mile high to leave the court.*'

Everybody looked at Alice.

'*I'm* not a mile high,' said Alice.

'You are,' said the King.

'Nearly two miles high,' added the Queen.

'Well, I shan't go, at any rate,' said Alice: 'besides, that's not a regular rule: you invented it just now.'

'It's the oldest rule in the book,' said the King.

'Then it ought to be Number One,' said Alice.

The King turned pale, and shut his note-book hastily.

'Consider your verdict,' he said to the jury, in a low trembling voice.

'There's more evidence to come yet, please your Majesty,' said the White Rabbit, jumping up in a great hurry; 'this paper has just been picked up.'

'What's in it?' said the Queen.

'I haven't opened it yet,' said the White Rabbit, 'but it seems to be a letter, written by the prisoner to — to somebody.'

'It must have been that,' said the King, 'unless it was written to nobody, which isn't usual, you know.'

'Who is it directed to?' said one of the jurymen.

'It isn't directed at all,' said the White Rabbit; 'in fact, there's nothing written on the *outside*.' He unfolded the paper as he spoke, and added 'It isn't a letter, after all: it's a set of verses.'

'Are they in the prisoner's handwriting?' asked another of the jurymen.

'No, they're not,' said the White Rabbit, 'and that's the queerest thing about it.' (The jury all looked puzzled.)

'He must have imitated somebody else's hand,' said the King. (The jury all brightened up again.)

'Please your Majesty,' said the Knave, 'I didn't write it, and they can't prove I did: there's no name signed at the end.'

'If you didn't sign it,' said the King, 'that only makes the matter worse. You *must* have meant some mischief, or else you'd have signed your name like an honest man.'

There was a general clapping of hands at this: it was the first really clever thing the King had said that day.

'That *proves* his guilt,' said the Queen.

'It proves nothing of the sort!' said Alice. 'Why, you don't even know what they're about!'

'Read them,' said the King.

The White Rabbit put on his spectacles. 'Where shall I begin, please your Majesty?' he asked.

'Begin at the beginning,' the King said gravely, 'and go on till you come to the end: then stop.'

These were the verses the White Rabbit read:—

> '*They told me you had been to her,*
> *And mentioned me to him:*
> *She gave me a good character,*
> *But said I could not swim.*
>
> *He sent them word I had not gone*
> *(We know it to be true):*
> *If she should push the matter on,*
> *What would become of you?*
>
> *I gave her one, they gave him two,*
> *You gave us three or more;*
> *They all returned from him to you,*
> *Though they were mine before.*
>
> *If I or she should chance to be*
> *Involved in this affair,*
> *He trusts to you to set them free,*
> *Exactly as we were.*

> *My notion was that you had been*
> *(Before she had this fit)*
> *An obstacle that came between*
> *Him, and ourselves, and it.*
>
> *Don't let him know she liked them best,*
> *For this must ever be*
> *A secret, kept from all the rest,*
> *Between yourself and me.'*

'That's the most important piece of evidence we've heard yet,' said the King, rubbing his hands; 'so now let the jury —'

'If any one of them can explain it,' said Alice, (she had grown so large in the last few minutes that she wasn't a bit afraid of interrupting him,) 'I'll give him sixpence. *I* don't believe there's an atom of meaning in it.'

The jury all wrote down on their slates, '*She* doesn't believe there's an atom of meaning in it,' but none of them attempted to explain the paper.

'If there's no meaning in it,' said the King, 'that saves a world of trouble, you know, as we needn't try to find any. And yet I don't know,' he went on, spreading out the verses on his knee, and looking at them with one eye; 'I seem to see some meaning in them, after all. "*— said I could not swim —*" you can't swim, can you?' he added, turning to the Knave.

The Knave shook his head sadly. 'Do I look like it?' he said. (Which he certainly did *not*, being made entirely of cardboard.)

'All right, so far,' said the King, and he went on muttering over the verses to himself: '"*We know it to be true—*" that's the jury, of course — "*I gave her one, they gave him two*
5 —" why, that must be what he did with the tarts, you know—'

But, it goes on "*they all returned from him to you*,"' said Alice.

'Why, there they are!' said the
10 King triumphantly, pointing to the tarts on the table. 'Nothing can be clearer than *that*. Then again —"*before she had*
15 *this fit —*" you never had fits, my dear, I think?' he said to the Queen.

'Never!' said the Queen furiously, throwing an ink-
20 stand at the Lizard as she spoke. (The unfortunate little Bill had left off writing on his slate with one finger, as he found it made no mark; but he now hastily began again, using the ink, that was trickling down his face, as long as it lasted.)

25 'Then the words don't *fit* you,' said the King, looking round the court with a smile. There was a dead silence.

'It's a pun!' the King added in an offended tone, and everybody laughed. 'Let the jury consider their verdict,' the King said, for about the twentieth time that day.

'No, no!' said the Queen. 'Sentence first — verdict afterwards.'

'Stuff and nonsense!' said Alice loudly. 'The idea of having the sentence first!'

'Hold your tongue!' said the Queen, turning purple.

'I won't!' said Alice.

'Off with her head!' the Queen shouted at the top of her voice. Nobody moved.

'Who cares for you?' said Alice, (she had grown to her full size by this time.) 'You're nothing but a pack of cards!'

At this the whole pack rose up into the air, and came flying down upon her: she gave a little scream, half of fright and half of anger, and tried to beat them off, and found herself lying on the bank, with her head in the lap of her sister, who was gently brushing away some dead leaves that had fluttered down from the trees upon her face.

'Wake up, Alice dear!' said her sister; 'Why, what a long sleep you've had!'

'Oh, I've had such a curious dream!' said Alice, and she told her sister, as well as she could remember them, all these strange Adventures of hers that you have just been reading about; and when she had finished, her sister kissed her, and said, 'It *was* a curious dream, dear, certainly: but now run in to your tea; it's getting late.' So Alice got up and ran off, thinking while she ran, as well she might, what a wonderful dream it had been.

But her sister sat still just as she left her, leaning her head on her hand, watching the setting sun, and thinking of little Alice and all her wonderful Adventures, till she too began dreaming after a fashion, and this was her dream: —

First, she dreamed of little Alice herself, and once again the tiny hands were clasped upon her knee, and the bright eager eyes were looking up into hers — she could hear the very tones of her voice, and see that queer little toss of her head to keep back the wandering hair that *would* always get into her eyes — and still as she listened, or seemed to listen, the whole place around her became alive with the strange creatures of her little sister's dream.

The long grass rustled at her feet as the White Rabbit hurried by — the frightened Mouse splashed his way through the neighbouring pool — she could hear the rattle of the teacups as the March Hare and his friends shared their never-ending meal, and the shrill voice of the Queen ordering off her unfortunate guests to execution — once more the pig-baby was sneezing on the Duchess's knee, while plates and dishes crashed around it — once more the shriek of the Gryphon, the squeaking of the Lizard's slate-pencil, and the choking of the suppressed guinea-pigs, filled the air, mixed up with the distant sobs of the miserable Mock Turtle.

So she sat on, with closed eyes, and half believed herself in Wonderland, though she knew she had but to open them again, and all would change to dull reality — the grass would be only rustling in the wind, and the pool rippling to the waving of the reeds — the rattling teacups would change to tinkling sheep-bells, and the Queen's shrill cries to the voice of the shepherd boy — and the sneeze of the baby, the shriek of the Gryphon, and all the other queer noises, would change (she knew) to the confused clamour of the busy farm-yard — while the lowing of the cattle in the distance would take the place of the Mock Turtle's heavy sobs.

Lastly, she pictured to herself how this same little sister of hers would, in the after-time, be herself a grown woman; and how she would keep, through all her riper years, the simple and loving heart of her childhood: and how she would gather about her other little children, and make *their* eyes bright and eager with many a strange tale, perhaps even with the dream of Wonderland of long ago: and how she would feel with all their simple sorrows, and find a pleasure in all their simple joys, remembering her own child-life, and the happy summer days.

THE END

I. *Down the Rabbit-Hole*

p. 1.

1　1-2　**her sister**「彼女のお姉さん」この童話の Alice のモデルとなった実際の Alice Liddell の姉は Lorina Liddell という。

　　8　**sleepy**　この日はとても暑い日で、眠かったので Alice はできるだけ眠らないように努めていた。

　　9　**daisy-chain**　「ひな菊の花輪」

2　1　**out of the way** = unusual, extraordinary.

　　7　**started to her feet** = suddenly jumped up.

　12　**pop down a large rabbit-hole**　「大きなうさぎ穴にひょいと跳びこむ」

　23　**make out** = see (where she was arriving at).

3　6　**think nothing of tumbling down stairs**　「二階から階段をころがり落ちたってなんとも思わない」

　　9　**Which was very likely true**　「屋根から落ちたらそれこそものが言えるどころではないだろう」

　23-4　**fall right *through* the earth**「落ちて行って地球を突き抜ける」

　26　**Antipathies**　Alice は antipodes「対蹠（せき）地」（地球の正反対の地）と間違えたのであろう。

5　5　**Oh my ears and whiskers**「おや、これは大変だ」p.2, 1, 2 の Oh dear! や Oh, my God などと同意だが、ここはうさぎの言葉だから、その特徴である長い耳とほほひげを引き合いにだしたもの。

　11-2　**all the way down one side and up the other, trying every door**「わざわざ広間の手前から反対側まで行ったり来たりして、とびらというとびらを引っ張ってみた」

7　14　**disagree with you** = make you ill.

　17　**cherry-tart**「サクランボ入りの小さいタルト」

8　1-3　**it might end ... in my going out altogether, like a candle**「しまいには、私がろうそくのように全て消えてなくなるかも知れない」

　18　**leave off (crying)** = stop (crying).

　23-4　**a game of croquet she was playing against herself**「自分自身を相手にやっていたクロウケイ遊戯」"croquet" 芝生の上で木球を打って6本の鉄の hoops の中を通過させて勝負を争う一種の遊戯。

　27-8　**there's hardly enough of me left to make *one* respectable person**「一人前の人間の大きさもない」

9　14　**had got ... into the way of ...**「... する癖がついてしまった」

　18　**set to work** = began to eat vigorously.

II *The Pool of Tears*

11	16	**she might well say this**「彼女がそういうのも当たり前です（9フィート以上も背があるんですから）」
	20	**reaching half down the hall**「広間の床の半（なか）程まで達する」
	27	**savage** = (*colloq.*) angry.
12	12-	**I almost think I can remember feeling a little different**「思い出してみると少々違っているような気がしたようだわ」
13	15-6	**Multiplication Table**「掛け算表」ただし英語では 12 ×12=144 まである。
	16	**doesn't signify** = doesn't matter.
	20	**How doth the little**——キャロルはパロディが得意で、これも 'How doth the little busy bee'で始まる Isaac Watts(1674-1748)の教訓歌 *Divine Songs for Children* の中で "Against Idleness and Mischief" と題する歌のパロディーである。
14	4	***jaws*** = mouth.
	8-9	**next to no toys**=scarcely any toys.
15	19	**bathing machines**「移動更衣室」
16	3	**made out** = saw or understood.
	25-6	**A mouse——of a mouse...O mouse** これらはラテン語の格変化の英訳である。
17	2-3	**William the Conqueror**「ウィリアム征服王」もと Duke of Normandy であったが、1066 年に英国を征服して、英国の初代の王ウィリアム一世となった。今から 940 年以上前のことであるから、そんな年をとったねずみがいる筈がない。
	5	**Où est ma chatte ?** = (F.) Where is my cat?
	8	**all over**「からだ中」
	21	**to nurse**「抱いてやると」
		capital = (*colloq.*) excellent.
18	7	**terrier**「テリア」小型の猟犬で、狐やうさぎの穴の中まで入って行って、これを捕える。
19	10	**there were a Duck and a Dodo, a Lory and an Eaglet**「かもにドードー鳥、ひいんこに子わしがいた」 'dodo' は、がちょうほどの大きさの鳥で、かつてインド洋の Mauritius 島に住んでいたが今は絶滅した。'lory' はひいんこ科の羽毛の美しい小鳥。Charles Lutwidge Dodgson がここで Dodo となって顔を出している。最初の Duck はやはりその舟遊びに一緒に行った作者の友人 Canon Duckworth を諷している。Lory は Alice の姉の Lorina, Eaglet は妹の Edith である。

III. *A Caucus-Race and a Long Tale*

20		**Caucus -Race**「党大会レース」
		Long Tale「長い尾話(おはなし)」
	23	**the driest thing** 'dry'の「乾いた」と「無味乾燥の」の両意にかけたもの。

21	5	**ugh!**「うっ！」二十日ネズミの話はあまりにも堅苦しい文章なので、Loryも嫌悪の嘆声を発した。
	11	**declared for him**「ウィリアム征服王に味方すると宣言した」
	28	**I move that the meeting adjourn**「この会合が散会されんことを動議として提出します」
22	21	**There was no One, two, three, and away!**「一、二、三、それっ！なんていう合図も全然なかった」
23	3-4	**the position . . . in the pictures of him**「絵でよく見るシェイクスピアの姿勢」
	16	**one a-piece**「一人につき一つ」
25	1	**C and D** もちろん Cats and Dogs.
	5	**tail** l.3 'tale'にかけたしゃれ。
	7	**kept on puzzling**「頭をひねりつづけた」
26	1	**Fury**「狂暴」という名の野良犬だが、このねずみのしっぽの形をした文章は韻(rhyme)を踏んでいて、詩形を備えている。即ち Fury said to a *mouse,*/ That he met in the *house.* その他 *denial*：*trial*/*cur*：*sir*/*jury*：*Fury*.
	10-11	**take no denial**「いやおう言わさぬ」
	27-9	**wasting our breath**「むだなことばを費す」
	36-9	**I'll try the whole cause**「この訴訟は一切合切おれが一人で裁く」
27	1	**You are not attending!** 「あなたは聞いていませんね」
	3-4	**you had got to the fifth bend**「第五番目の曲がり目へ来たんだわね」第五番目の曲がり目は p.26 のねずみのしっぽを見ると、'whole cause, and condemn' あたりになる。
	5	**I had *not*!**「来ない！」の 'not' が l. 7 の 'knot'「(しっぽの) もつれ」と pun になっている。
	20	**What a pity (it is that) it wouldn't stay!**
	26	**You're enough to try the patience of an oyster**「そんなにおっしゃると、辛抱強い牡蠣(かき)だって怒りますわよ」
28	7	**after the birds** = run after the birds.

IV *The Rabbit Sends in a Little Bill*

	29	**The Rabbit Sends In a Little Bill** うさぎが勘定書を差し出すのは、アリスが魔法のびんの中身を飲んだ代金を請求する意味と、p.35, l. 6 の "Oh! So Bill's got to come down the chimney, has he?" というアリスの独り言の中の Bill という名前のとかげにひっかけたもの。つまり「うさぎさん小さいビルを送り込む」にひっかけた pun である。
	4-5	**Oh my dear paws! Oh my fur and whiskers** 驚きを表す感嘆詞として、うさぎに縁のある言葉をおもしろく引き合いに出したもの。
	5-6	**as sure as ferrets are ferrets**「白いたちが白いたちであるようにたしかに」とは「全

		くたしかに」の意。
	15	**Mary Ann** 二語だが一人の名前。
30	1	**W. RABBIT** 白うさぎだから White の略と解してよいだろう。
	7	**going messages**「お使いに行く」
	11	**Coming in a minute, nurse!**「乳母（ばあ）や、すぐ行くわ」
	16	**had found her way into ...**「〜に入って来ていた」
31	11	**tried the effect of lying down**「横になってみたらどうかとためしてみた」
	17-8	**had now had its full effect**「利き目はもう充分であった」
32	2-3	**that there ought!**「ほんとうに！」前に自分が言った言葉を強く肯定する言い方。
	7	**one way** = in one respect.
	13-14	**talking first one side and then the other**「自分になって話したり、相手になって話したりして」
33	17	**cucumber-frame**「きゅうりの温室」
	19	**Pat** 下男の名前でいかにも田舎者らしく、方言を使っている。
	23	**yer honour** 'yer は your の方言あるいは卑語。 'your honour' は相手への敬称語で、ここでは「だんな様」位。
34	4	**goose** = (*colloq.*) fool.
	22	**made out the words**「次の言葉を聞き取った」
	23	**I hadn't to bring but one** = I had to bring only one.「おれは一つしか持ってくる必要はなかったんだ。」
	26-7	**particular**「やかましい」「こうるさい」
35	9-10	**I wouldn't be in Bill's place for a good deal**「いくらもらっても私はビルの役はごめんだわ」
36	4	**a deal** = (*colloq.*) a great deal, a lot.
	6	**Jack-in-the-box**「びっくり箱」
		up I goes 'goes' は 俗語 か方言で通常は go.
37	5	**guinea-pig**「モルモット」
38	3-4	**made believe to worry it**「それを振りまわすふりをした」
	9	**cart-horse**「荷馬車馬」
39	12	**tricks**「芸当」
	24	**might as well** (= had better) look and see「見てみようかな（と）」
40	2	**hookah**「水ぎせる」

V *Advice from a Caterpillar*

42	14	**chrysalis**「（特にちょうの）さなぎ」
	24	**short**「ぶっきらぼうな」「そっけない」
	24-5	**drew herself up**「きっとなった」「そり身になった」

43	14-5	**puffed away**「水ぎせるをぷかぷか吹かしていた」	
	25	***"You are old, Father William"*** これは英国の Lake Poets の一人 Robert Southey(1774—1843)の教訓詩 "The Old Man's Comforts, and How He Gained Them" のパロディーである。	
44	3	**stand on your head**「逆立ちする」	
	11	**turned a back-somersault in at the door**「戸口から後ろへとんぼ返りをして入った」	
	16	***a couple*** = a couple of boxes = two boxes.	
45	6	**took to the law**「法律に没頭した」	
	7	**argued each case with my life**「訴訟事件ごとに女房と議論した」	
	12	**balanced an eel on the end of your nose** うなぎは 'slippery as an eel' という成句がある位ぬるぬるとすべっこいのに、それを鼻の先でバランスをとってあやつるとは神業。
	15	**give yourself airs**「威張る」	
48	15	**it had struck her foot**「下あごが足にぶつかった」'it' = her chin.	
	19	**the other bit** = the left-hand bit.	
50	18	**to invent something**「うそをつこうと」	
51	24-5	**It was so long since she had been anything near the right size, that it felt quite strange at first**「彼女は当たり前の背丈に近かった時からもう大分経っていたので、最初は全く変な感じだった」	

VI *Pig and Pepper*

53	9	**powdered hair**「髪粉をふりかけた頭髪」（１８世紀ごろ hair-powder という芳香のある白い粉末をかつらに振りかけることが流行したが、この習慣が下男にも残っているようである。	
	16	**croquet** Chapter VIII にくわしい。	
54	4	**no sort of**「どんな...も（全然）ない」	
55	7	**he might answer questions**「質問に答えるぐらいしてくれてもよさそうなものだ」	
	26	**with variations**「文句を変えて」	
	21-2	**to fix on one** = to choose a subject.	
58	2	**mind what you're doing!**「そんなことはなさらないで！」	
	3-4	**there goes his *precious* nose**「あれ、赤ちゃんの大切な鼻がとれてしまうわ」	
	6	**If everybody minded their own business**「もし世の中の人が皆他人のことに余計な口出しをしなければ」	
	7-8	**the world would go round a deal faster than it does**「この世の中の物事は今よりずっと円滑に進行するだろうに」	
	11-2	**Just think of what work it would make with the day and night!**「そうすれば、昼と夜がどうなるか考えてごらんなさいよ！」	
	13	**turn round on its (own) axis**「自転する」	

	17	**to take the hint**｜「(ほのめかされて) それと感づく」	
	21	**never could abide figures**｜「数字は我慢ができない」	
59	24	**doubling itself up**｜「からだを二重に折り曲げ」	
	26-	**it was as much as she could do to hold it**｜「それを抱いているのが精一杯であった」	
60	15	**turn-up nose**｜「(鼻の穴が) 上を向いた鼻」	
61	7	**neither more nor less than** = literally｜「正真正銘」「とりも直さず」	
	15	**who might do very well as pigs**｜「豚としてぴったり似合いそうな」	
	13-5	**a Hatter: and ... a March Hare ...: they're both mad**　very mad の意味で、'as mad as hatter' とか 'as mad as a March hare' という成句があるが、ここの Hatter も March hare もこれらの成句から著者が作り出した人物である。	
64	8	**much the most interesting** = much more interesting.	

Ⅶ　*A Mad Tea-Party*

66	3	**Dormouse**｜「やまね」(りすとねずみとの中間の動物)
67	3	**personal remarks**　「人身攻撃」
68	22	**the works**　「(時計などの) 機械部分」
70	3	**It's *him***｜「時は『男』だよ」前行に『時』を人間扱いして大文字で表わしている。
	9	**beat time**｜「拍子を正しくとる」
71	2	***what you're at*** = what you are engaged in.
72	2	***between whiles***｜「合間に」「時折」
	4-5	**as the things get used up**｜「お茶道具が使い切られてしまうので」
	9	**I vote ...** = I vote that ... 'to vote'=(*colloq.*) to suggest; to propose.
73	1	**treacle**〔英〕「糖みつ」(砂糖精製の時に生じる黒色の残液。パンに塗ったりするとおいしいので、子供が食べすぎると病気になるとおどかされる)
74	2	***one*** = a treacle-well.
	5	**they were learning to draw**｜「彼女達は絵を描く勉強をしていたんです」この動詞には少なくとも (1)「(絵を) 描く」と (2)「(水を) くみ上げる」の両意がある。
	10-1	**let's all move one place on**｜「皆ひとつずつ席をずらそう」
	16-7	**worse off** = in worse circumstances｜「より悪い状態に」
	21	**where did they draw the treacle from?**　この 'draw' の意味については、おそらくアリスは依然として「描く」の意にとって、定形のない液体の treacle をどこから描くのか、と聞いたのだろう。それを次行で帽子屋は (2) の「汲(く)み上げる」という意味にとっているが、この方がむしろ自然。
	27	**well in**｜「うんと深いところに」
75	13	**muchness**　「沢山」の意味だが、特に 'much of a muchness'(「似たりよったり」)という成句として用いられる。

VIII *The Queen's Croquet-Ground*

77		**Croquet-Ground** 'croquet' とは、芝生のあちこちに鉄の細い棒を曲げて作った6本の柱門（hoops）を立て、木球（wooden balls）を木づち（mallet）で打って門柱の中を通過させて勝負を争う遊戯（lawn-game）。
	17	**for bringing the cook tulip-roots**「料理人のためにチューリップの根をもってきてやったため」
	20-1	**checked himself**「のどまで出かかった言葉をおさえた」
78	14-5	**upon their faces**「うつぶせになって」
	19	**First came ten soldiers** この行列の 'soldiers' も 'ten courtiers' (l. 21-2) も、'royal children' (= 'the little dears') (l. 24) も、'King' と 'Queen' (l. 27) も全部、トランプの組札（suits）を人間扱いしている。
	19	**ten soldiers carrying clubs** この10人の兵士たちはトランプの clubs の ace から ten までの組札を指している。
	23	**two and two**「二人ずつ組んで」
79	3	**Knave of Hearts**「ハートのジャック」
	20	**so please your Majesty**「おそれながら」
	25	**were lying**「平伏していた」
80	12	**Turn them over!**「あの者どもをひっくり返せ！」
81	1	**You shan't be beheaded!**「お前たちの首は切らせはしないわ！」
82	24	**tumbling up against each other**「ころびそうになって、おたがいにぶつかり合った」
83	1-2	**stand on their hands and feet**「手と足を地につけて（アーチを造る）」
	2	**arches** hoops のこと。
	4-5	**getting its body tucked away . . . under her arm**「フラミンゴの身体を自分のうでの下に抱え込むこと」
84	24	**there was enough of it now in sight**「もうこれだけ見せれば十分」
85	5-6	**I should have croqueted the Queen's hedgehog**「（もし逃げ出さなければ）女王のはりねずみをはね飛ばしたものを」
	24	**A cat may look at a king** これは「ねこでも王様を見られる」から「どんなに身分の低い者でも貴人の前でそれ相当の権利はある」「見るのは自由」などの意に用いる諺。しかし、ここではずばり原義通りであるのが面白い。
86	11-2	**the look of things**「この有様」
87	21-2	**he wasn't going to begin at his time of life**「こんな年齢でそんなことを始めるつもりはない」
	26	**in less than no time**「直ちに」
	27	**all round**「まんべんなんく」「みんな同じように」
88	9	**up and down**「あちこちと」

IX *The Mock Turtle's Story*

89	14	**camomile**「かみつれ」（キク科の薬用植物でにがい健胃剤を作る）
		barley-sugar「大麦糖」（昔大麦を煮た汁で砂糖を煮詰めて作った一種のキャンディ）
90	16-7	**by way of keeping up the conversation**「会話をつないでいくために」
	19-20	**'tis love, that makes the world go round** これはフランスの諺。
	25-6	**Take care of the sense, and the sounds will take care of themselves**「意味に気をつけよ、そうすれば音も自ずからきまる」'Take care of the pence, and the pounds will take care of themselves'（小銭を大切にすれば大金はおのずから集まる、つまり小事をゆるがせにしなければ大事はおのずからうまくゆく）という英国18世紀の有名な諺をもじったもの。
91	8	**bite**「かむ」と「(からしなどが) ひりひりする」の両義がある。
	12	**putting things** = expressing things.
	17	**mine**「鉱山」と「私のもの」の二意に掛けてある。
	22	**Be what you would seem to be**「自分がかく思われたいと望むものになれ」
	23-4	**Never imagine yourself ... otherwise** この文章は意味がありそうで判読しようとするとちんぷんかんぷんであり、意味ありげにみせかけたいわゆる perfect jargon である。
92	3	**to** = compared with
	16-7	**as much right ... as pigs have to fly**（お前さんの考える権利は）「豚の持っている飛ぶ権利と同じ程度だね」とは、実際豚は飛べないから、「お前さんには考える権利はない」という意。
	28	**and that in about half no time**「しかもすぐにだ」
94	7	**Gryphon** ギリシア神話に出てくる怪獣で、ライオンの胴体にわしの頭と翼を持っている。Scythia に住んでその地の黄金を守ると信じられた。
	11	**see after**「～を世話する」「～を監督する」
95	5	**never executes nobody** 'nobody' は anybody と言うべきところ。
	15-6	**hasn't got no sorrow**「悲しいことなんかなにもねえんだ」'no' は any とすべきところ。
	19-20	**she wants for to know** = she wants to know. 'for' をつけるのは古体か方言か、或は無教育者の言葉づかい。
96	2	**Hjckrrh!** これは Gryphon のくしゃみか何かだろう。
	11	**Tortoise** 陸がめで、これと同源語の turtle は普通海がめ。
97	3	**taught us** これは Tortoise との言葉遊び。
	19	**day-school** = an elementary week-day school, as distinguished from a *Sunday school*—(O. E. D.)
	21	**extras**「課外授業」（別に授業料がかかる）
	28	**—extra**「左記は別勘定」
98	6	**Reeling and Writhing**「よろめき方ともだえ方」もちろん reading and writing（読

  み方と書き方）をもじったもの。

  8-9 **Ambition, Distraction, Uglification, and Derision** addition（寄せ算）、subtraction（引き算）、multiplication（掛け算）、division（割り算）、をもじったもの。

  22 **Mystery history**（歴史）をもじったもの。

  24 **Seaography** geography（地理）をもじったもの。
    Drawling drawing（図画）のしゃれ。

  26 **Stretching**「身体の伸ばし方」これは sketching（スケッチ法）のもじり。

  27 **Fainting in Coils**「とぐろを巻いての失神法」は painting in oil（油絵の描き方）のもじりで、conger-eel（あなご）のやりそうな動作にしたもの。

99 6 **Laughing and Grief** Latin and Greek のもじり。

  15 **lessen**「減ってゆく」これは前行の lesson に掛けたしゃれ。

X *The Lobster Quadrille*

100   **Quadrille** = a square dance, of French origin, usually performed by four couples, and containing five sections or figures, each of which is a complete dance in itself. —(*O.E.D.*)「カドリル」

  1-2 **drew ... across his eyes**「～で眼をふいた」

101 1-2 **set to partners**（ダンスで）「相手と向かいあいになる」

  3 **retire in same order**「同じ順序で後ろへもどる」

102 2 **the first figure**「第一段のフィギュア」'figure'=(in dancing) a set of evolutions or movements of a dance or a dancer; also, one of the divisions into which a set dance is divided.—(*O.E.D.*)

  9-10 **mark the time**「拍子をとる」

  16 *shingle*「じゃり浜」「小石の浜」

103 3 *scaly friend*「うろこのある友」（たらのこと）

  14 **I do so like** = I like very much.

  17 **dinn-** アリスは dinner と言うつもりだったのを途中でやめたもの。Mock Turtle はこれを地名とまちがえた。

  25 **wash off**「洗われて落ちる」

104 11 *It does the boots and shoes* shine と言えばよいところを 'does' のような漠然とした意味の語を使うことが日常の会話にはよくある。

  18 **blacking** 黒いくつ墨。

  21 **whiting** 'whiting' は通例「たら」の意だが、ここでは blacking（黒いくつ墨）に対して「白いくつ墨」の意をもたせたところがみそ。

  25 **Soles and eels**「ひらめとうなぎ」sole（くつの底皮）と heels（くつのかかと）にかけたもの。教育のない人たちの英語やCockney slangでは[h]音が落ちるから heels

			は eels になる。
105	1	**Keep back**「お控えなさい」	
	10	**with what porpoise!** porpoise' と purpose とのしゃれ。	
	26-8	**got to the part about her repeating ... and the words all coming different**「彼女が～を暗唱すると文句が皆ちがってきたという箇所に来た」	
106	15-7	**I might as well be at school at once**「(こんなことをするのなら) いっそ学校へ行っている方がましだわ」	
107	17	**position**「姿勢」	
	28	*had the dish*「皿をかじっていた」	
108	10	**only too glad**「ただただ喜んでそうした」	
109	2	*Game*「猟鳥獣の肉」	
	3	*two p* この 'p' は次行の '*ennyworth*' と一緒になって *pennyworth* となるべきものだが、ここでは 'two p' 'Soup' と韻をふませるために孤立している。	
	18-9	**carried on the breeze that followed them**「彼らの後から吹くそよ風に運ばれて」	

XI *Who Stole the Tarts?*

110	5	**in chains**「くさりにつながれて」これは前の 'the Knave' の状態を述べたもの。
	11	**get the trial done**「裁判を片づけてしまう」
	15	**court of justice**「裁判所」「法廷」
	19	**wig**「かつら」英国の裁判官は今でもかつらをつける習慣がある。
	24	**jury-box**「陪審員席」
111	7	**jurymen would have done just as well**「'jurymen' でも同じように間に合っただろう」
112	2	**A nice muddle their slates'll be in** = Their slates will be in a nice muddle.「あの石板(せきばん)はひどくごちゃごちゃになるだろう」
	4	**pencil**「石筆」
113	14-5	**reduced the answer to shillings and pence**「その答えを何シリング何ペンスに換算した」上の日付 (3:14, 3:15, 3:16) を合計すると 9:45 となる。これを著者がこの童話を書いた当時の英国の通貨に換算すると、1 shilling は 12 pence だったから、9 shillings 45 pence は twelve shillings nine pence(12/9)になる。
	27	**kept shifting from one foot to the other**「足を変えつづけた」
	28-	**bit a large piece out of his teacup**「自分の紅茶茶わんを一口大きくかみとった」
114	8	**I wish you wouldn't squeeze so**「そんなにぎゅうぎゅう押さないでほしいね」
115	5	**the twinkling of the tea**「お茶はきらめく(やらで)」
116	7	**tied up at the mouth with strings**「口のところをひもで結えられてあった」
	14	**stand down**「(法廷の)証人台から降りる」これをまた文字通りに解して、'I can't go no lower' (もうこれ以上は降りられません) と答えたのである。
	18	*sit* **down** 王も 'stand down' できないなら 'sit down' しろと、しゃれでやり返した。

117	13	**Shan't** = I shan't give my evidence.「いやです」口語で主語を省略することはよくある。
	18	**folding his arms**「うでを組んで」
	18-9	**frowning at the cook**「ひたいに八の字をよせて料理人をにらめつけながら」
	23	**Collar**「首輪をつけよ」
118	6-7	**fumbled over the list**「名簿を不器用な手つきでめくりながら」

XII *Alice's Evidence*

119	1	**Here!** = Yes!
	1-2	**in the flurry of the moment**「とっさのことにうろたえて」
	5-6	**the crowd below**「下の群衆」傍聴人たちのこと。
	7	**globe**「金魚ばち」
	24-	**it would be *quite* (of) as much use in the trial one way up as the other** (way up)「裁判ではこっち（頭）が上でも、あっち（しっぽ）が上なのと役に立つ度合いは全く同じだろう」とは、前後関係から「どっちが上でも全くどうでもいいことだろう」という意味になる。
121	6-7	**making faces at him** = making grimaces or frowning at the King.
	9	**went on to himself** = went on to say to himself.
123	14	***character*** （前の雇主が使用人に与える）「人物証明書」「推せん状」
124	10	**rubbing his hands**「両手をもみながら」（満足の表情）
	20	**a word of** = a lot of.
125	5-6	**what he did with the tarts**「タルト菓子を彼がどうしたか」
	25	**Then the words don't *fit* you**「ではこの文句はそなたには当てはまらぬな」
126	2-3	**Sentence first ―verdict afterwards**「宣告が先で、評決は後じゃ」
	11	**her full size** 元通りの大きさに戻ったこと
127	22	**after a fashion** = to some extent. この24行以下は、アリスのお姉さんのまどろみを通して、もう一度アリスの冒険のあらましをたどり、最後にこの不思議な国の夢物語に対するお姉さんの感想を述べてある。
128	2-3	**the wandering hair that would always get into her eyes.**（はらってもはらっても）「どうしても眼に入ろうとするほつれ毛」
	20	**had but to...**「（し）さえすればよい」

参考書目

(1) Roger Lancelyn Green (ed. with an intro.),   *Lewis Carroll : Alice's Adventures in*

Wonderland and Through the Looking-Glass (Oxford English Novels ; Oxford University Press, London, 1971).
(2)　河合祥一郎訳　『不思議の国のアリス』（角川文庫、東京：2010）

不思議の国のアリス
《ALICE'S ADVENTURES IN WONDERLAND》

2010年4月1日　第1刷発行
2020年3月10日　第8刷発行

原作者	Carroll, L.
注釈者	丸橋　良雄
	伊藤　佳世子
発行者	藤平　英一

発　行　所
英　光　社

〒113-0021　東京都文京区本駒込5-6-5　西明ビル1F
Tel・Fax　(03) 3827-5159　出版社コード 0609
info@eiko-sha.com

印刷・製本　(株)平河工業社

★落丁・乱丁はお取り替えいたします